OLD WHORE LIFE

Exploring the Shadow Side of Karma

Spiritual Musings – Volume 2

OREST STOCCO

OLD WHORE LIFE

ISBN 978-0-9879357-5-5

Edited by Penny Lynn Cates

Cover Design by Penny Lynn Cates

Dedicated to Carl Gustav Jung, whose luminous candle shone a light in the darkness of my being.

"The shadow by nature is difficult to apprehend.
It is dangerous, disorderly, and forever in hiding, as if the
light of consciousness would steal its very life."

MEETING THE SHADOW
The Hidden Power of the Dark Side of Human Nature

Connie Zweig and Jeremiah Abrams

A Word for My Reader

"Life is a journey of the self," Ascended Master St. Padre Pio told me; but—and this is a very big but!—no two selves are the same. *"Our bodily personalities seem identical,"* said the poet Rumi, *"but the globe of soul fruit we make, each is elaborately unique."* And so is our journey through life!

"Know thyself," said the Delphic Oracle in ancient Greece, a divine directive so essential that it led Socrates in Plato's *Apology* to announce to the world during his trial for corrupting the youth of Athens with his "seditious" philosophy that *"the unexamined life is not worth living."* But who has time to examine their life today? And if we do take time, which self do we examine, "our bodily personality" or our "globe of soul fruit"—our ego self or our spiritual self? And how do we go about examining our life?

Reflection. Taking time out—it doesn't have to be more than a few minutes a day—to reflect upon our life, whether we are happy with our day's efforts, in our work or in our personal life, where we could have done better, for what purpose are we doing what we do, loved a little more and hurt a little less, or been a little more considerate and less self-serving; these moments of self-reflection open the window on our soul, and we begin to get a sense of our "globe of soul fruit" and the *raison d'être* of our being.

My spiritual musings are a form of creative self-reflection. Whenever my Muse whispers another idea into my ear—like the disconcerting idea to write a book of spiritual musings on "old whore life," the capricious shadow side of karma that takes great pleasure in screwing us of our virtue—I take time out to reflect, and ponder, and muse; this is how I keep the window on my soul open, and hopefully my musings will inspire you to reflect upon your life and open a window on your soul.

At first blush the concept of "old whore life" may be unsettling, but I have employed this literary conceit to explore the shadow side of karma. The "old whore" does not want to be seen, and it takes great moral courage to look into the face of our own shadow; but with the gift of imagination a writer can transform reality into a deeper perception of what is, and musing after musing I inched my way closer into the heart of "old whore life."

St. Padre Pio, the gentle Master of Humility who suffered the painful wounds of Jesus for fifty years and who was channeled by a gifted sensitive for my spiritual healing sessions that became the heart of my novel *Healing with Padre Pio*, also told me that "life is a voyage of discovery," and I'd like to invite you to join me in the second edition of my spiritual musings as I explore the music within and the secrets of "old whore life"—the elusive, mysterious, and disturbing shadow side of karma.

Orest Stocco,
May 25, 2012
Bluewater, Georgian Bay

Table of Contents

1. A Delightful Little Coincidence

It wasn't earth shattering, or anything like that—though I have had coincidences that did shake me up!—but the other morning after I had just finished writing the final musing for the first edition of my spiritual musings (*Just Going with the Flow*), Penny, my life companion, reminded me that the anniversary of her sister's husband's death was coming up in a few days, and she suggested that I post a memorial tribute on Facebook.

It was a wonderful idea, seeing that I had just quoted him in the final spiritual musing of my first edition. *"Be not afraid to explore the music within,"* said Penny's brother-in-law, *"for at your command the orchestra is ready to perform."*

I love this quote. In one stroke of creative genius, this insight speaks to the essential directive of the Way. But this requires an explanation; so, if I may, let me probe what it means to "explore the music within" before I relate the little coincidence that I was blessed with when I posted my memorial tribute on Facebook for the author of this insight.

The Way is the omniscient guiding force of life, which all religions and spiritual paths recognize as Divine Spirit; and as I have illustrated in the first edition of my musings, the Way speaks to us in the language of life, just as it did in the above saying to not be afraid to explore the music within.

What, then, is the Way trying to tell us by exploring the music within? What is this music within? And how do we explore it?

Imagine if you will a stream of Divine Consciousness flowing out of the Godhead like an endless river of God's atoms flowing magnificently through all of God's creation, through all the spiritual worlds and down into the lower worlds of God, the Mental, Causal, Astral, and Physical Planes, and everywhere the River of God flows it creates life and encourages the atoms of God's Body to grow and evolve in Divine Consciousness, from the lowest life form all the way up to the highest life form in the reflective self of man; and imagine if you will the River of God flowing in an endless circle through life and back into itself in an endless circuitous flow, round, and round, and round creating new life and nurturing the atoms of God; and imagine the River of God breaking free of the endless circle of life and death and flowing back to the Godhead in another stream carrying with it all those atoms of God that have evolved enough in Divine Consciousness to break free of the circle of life and death and return back home to the Godhead.

In the teachings of the Way in every culture of the world this River of God is called by many names, but it is the Sound Current. This is the vital life force, which we commonly refer to as Divine Spirit, and it is both audible and visible.

In its audible form, Divine Spirit is heard as sound, from the chirp of a lowly cricket to the glorious sound of Beethoven's Ninth Symphony; and in its visible form Spirit is seen as light, from the magnificence of a rainbow in the sky to the euphoric insight of an epiphany. Saul of Tarsus was struck by both the Light and Sound of God on the road to Damascus where he was going to persecute Christians. The Sound and Light of Divine Spirit make up the River of God that flows through life and back to the Godhead.

The River of God flows through life and back into itself in an endless circle of life and death (karma and reincarnation) to give the atoms of God all the time they need to grow and evolve in Divine Consciousness until they are evolved enough to break free of the circle of life and death and jump into the River of God that flows back to the Godhead.

The River of Life that flows back into itself is the *natural way of spiritual evolution* through karma and reincarnation; and the River of Eternal Life that returns back to the Godhead is the *conscious way of spiritual evolution*, and every atom of God that is ready to break the cycle of karma and reincarnation must make the shift from the natural way of evolution to the conscious spiritual way of evolution (a shift from the River of Life into the River of Eternal Life); and we make this shift by listening to the "music" within—because the "music" within is our personal musical note, or individual spiritual vibration that makes up the Sound Current of the River of Eternal Life that flows back to the Godhead. In effect, our personal musical note is our "music within" and path back home to God.

By happy coincidence, I was listening to Mary Hynes yesterday, the host of CBC *Tapestry*, interviewing Victor L. Wooten, author of **The Music Lesson: A Spiritual Search**

3

for Growth Through Music, when I heard the language of life speaking through him.

Victor Wooten, believed to be the world's greatest bass player, said something that spoke the Way to me, which ties in beautifully with today's spiritual musing. One day a mysterious man called Uncle Clyde told Victor Wooten's fictional self (who is the narrator of his story *The Music Lesson)*, "Young man, it's time for you to catch up to your soul."

I knew instantly what he meant. I heard the "music" of Uncle Clyde's spiritual wisdom, which was his way of saying to Victor that it was time for him to tune into his own individual musical note!

Uncle Clyde saw that Victor was ready to make the shift in consciousness from the natural way of evolution (the River of Life) to the spiritual way of evolution (the River of Eternal Life) by catching the wave of his own musical note back home to the Godhead—which meant that it was time for Victor to "be" the "music within." It was Uncle Clyde's way of telling the gifted young Victor to make music his life, his path, his destiny.

Victor was puzzled by Uncle Clyde's comment, but the more he gave himself to Music, the more he resonated with his individual musical note, his inner self, which was his personal path back to the Godhead; and it was not a coincidence that he wrote a book on spiritual growth through Music!

It just so happens that Wooten's "music within" was his gift for music, just as Rumi's "music within" was his gift for poetry, Einstein's "music within" was his gift for theoretical physics, and Carl Jung's "music within" was his gift for individuating the consciousness of the Way—it

4

doesn't matter what one's "music within" may be, it is our path back home to the Godhead, and connecting with the "music within" is what life is all about.

In effect, we are all trying to break out of the fast flowing currents of the River of Life that keeps flowing back into itself and shift into the River of Eternal Life that flows back to the Godhead; but to make this shift we have to first "hear" the music within, and then we have to "be" the music!

Now I'd like to share the coincidence that I experienced the other morning. When Penny suggested that I post a memorial tribute to her sister's husband, I went on Facebook and posted my tribute, along with his personal motto *("be not afraid to explore the music within, for at your command the orchestra is ready to perform")* that spoke the directive of the Way—which is to explore the music within; but no sooner did I press the send key and his wife appeared on the Facebook chat line!

She couldn't have had time to read my tribute to her husband, because no sooner did I post it and she popped up on the chat line; so I sent her a message telling her that Penny and I had just posted a memorial tribute to her husband, and she quickly responded that she would read it and get back to us; which she did.

What a delightful little coincidence to start my day!

2. What Is the Sound of God?

I woke up this morning around 4 A. M. with a question on my mind: WHAT IS THE SOUND OF GOD? Within seconds, I heard the answer: LOVE.

I knew that this was given to me for a reason, so I got up and went to my writing room to write out my question and answer in my notebook, and then I went back to bed; but I couldn't sleep. How could I?

My mind was wide-awake. I had to get up. I put on a pot of coffee and booted my computer. I had to do a spiritual musing…

I know next to nothing about music. When I went to St. Edward's Separate School in my hometown an accordion teacher from Thunder Bay came to our school to see if anyone wanted to take music lessons. I enrolled, but I didn't take to the accordion; especially with all the ribbing that I got from my brothers. "Oompupa, oompupa," they teased me.

I can't play a musical instrument, but I love to whistle. One of my painting customers who heard me whistling every morning while I painted the exterior of her house called me "the happy painter." And I love to sing also, but only when I'm alone.

I have a terrible memory for songs, so I often make up my own words, which makes for an interesting twist on the songs I sing. One time I was poking fun at the interminable angst of country music and abandoned to my creative spirit and created a whole new genre that I dubbed *New Age Country!*

Obviously, I have a song in my soul. Maybe that's why I was so intrigued by the question that I woke up with this morning. I hardly had time to think of the answer before it came to me, so obviously I knew that the answer was love; but what does this mean?

I've had too many experiences of these extraordinary moments that are called coincidences to believe they are brought about by random chance, so why have I experienced all these little coincidences that have to do with music ever since I brought the first edition of my spiritual musings to closure with the final entry, "Being the Music"?

If the sound of God is love, it must follow that the love we have and give to others must be the music that God plays through us; which makes us God's musical instruments!

This takes "being the music" to a whole new level. I have a glimpse of what this new level is, but I have to approach it gently…

Let us imagine that we are all musical instruments of God, and love is the music that God plays through us.

Rumi said, "*These leaves, our bodily personalities, seem identical, but the globe of soul-fruit we make, each is elaborately unique.*" We all seem the same on the outside, but on the inside we are all unique.

In "Being the Music," I wrote that we have to connect with our inner self to "be" the music, and we connect with our inner self by finding our own path, and our path would be what we love to do—like the poet who loves to write poetry, the artist who loves to paint, the teacher who loves to teach, the doctor who loves to heal, the singer who loves to sing, and the musician who loves to play music. The actor Alan Arkin, who loves acting and starred in one of my favorite movies, *Catch 22*, said on the CBC Radio show Q, "We are what we do," but unless we love what we do we are never satisfied.

Loving what we do gives us satisfaction. Satisfaction makes us feel complete, and the more satisfaction we get in what we do, the more whole we feel; and the more whole we feel, the happier we are. Do you see where my Muse is going with this?

As instruments of God, we are all unique; and being unique, as all musical instruments are different from each other, so too do we all make a different sound; *and yet, the music is the same sound of love!*

It doesn't take a great leap of logic to see that the essence of happiness is love, and that love is the sound of our own life if we dare to live it; but this is the challenge, isn't it?

Life can be, and often is cruel. This is why I see life as an "old whore" that loves to screw us of our virtue every chance she gets. I say this because I know how hard it can be to live our own life. When Frank Sinatra sang his signature song "My Way", he spoke for everyone who had the courage to get "old whore life" off their back; but if one succeeds, the rewards will by far outweigh all the hardships that one has to endure to get "there". And where is "there" if not in God's Orchestra, playing to the sound of God's love?

This reminds me of Johanna Schneller's column FAME GAME in the *Globe and Mail* last Saturday (*June

18, 2011), an interview with Maria Bello, "an actress who's never afraid of the dark." "Sometimes when I've made a mistake with Jack" (her ten-year old son), says Maria Bello, "I think, `O dear God, he's going to be in therapy for the rest of his life.' I'm finding that the only thing I can do is fully be myself. Whoever I am, wherever I am. And teach him that's the most important thing for him as well. Be yourself. Walk your path, nobody else's."

What intuitive wisdom! Maria Bello gave her young son the best advice that a parent can give to their child. Like Polonius said to his son Laertes in Shakespeare's play *Hamlet* as he boarded his ship to France, "This above all to thine own self be true," because when you are true to yourself you are not in the audience listening to the music of life; you are playing in God's Orchestra!

3. Sitting on the John

Yesterday afternoon when I came home from an outside painting job that I was doing in Tiny Beaches on the shores of Georgian Bay because it had started to rain, I felt nature's call and picked up my May 2011 issue of ZOOMER magazine because I hadn't gone through all of the articles yet, and I was sitting on the John negotiating an "expression" when the language of life sang the most piercing little tune in my ear when I read what Debbie Papadakis, founder of the Hypno Healing Institute was quoted saying, ***"The way you do one thing is the way you do everything."***

The John is one of my favorite places to read. In fact, I often go to the John at the slightest hint of an "expression" just to read. I prefer magazines to books, because I can read an entire article in the John, which leaves me doubly satisfied; but if I don't have a magazine to peruse I'll bring a book and read a whole chapter. Sometimes I read the newspaper.

I discovered ZOOMER magazine while waiting to get my hair cut at The Corner Cut Salon in Elmvale two years ago. A barber used to cut my hair when I lived up north, but since Penny and I relocated to Georgian Bay seven years ago I've been going to the same hairstylist at the Corner Cut Salon because I love the way she cuts my curly hair, and as I leafed through the Special Collector's Issue of the October 2010 ZOOMER magazine, with the world's best known environmentalist David Suzuki on the cover, I got the strongest nudge to reconnect with the world of magazines.

My life was much too demanding the last seven years for me to read the magazines I used to read every month, but as I perused ZOOMER while waiting to get my hair cut I felt a very strong tug to reconnect with the currents of daily life, and that familiar feeling of excitement possessed me as it always did whenever I came home from Chapters in Thunder Bay with a fresh stack of my favorite magazines to read.

"Go with life and the living, not the dead and dying," said Jesus, in Glenda Green's book *Love Without End, Jesus Speaks*, which Padre Pio recommended for me to read in one of my spiritual healing sessions; and I knew that by going with life and the living Jesus meant that life is forever unfolding in consciousness, with the best and brightest and most creative leading the way—and which I instantly recognized as I perused ZOOMER in The Corner Cut Salon a year and a half before I read Glenda Green's book!

I heard the Call, as it were. The Call is the silent voice of the Way that beckons Soul to a higher purpose, which always excites me because it feels like going around a new corner in life. I didn't know then what this new corner held in store for me, but it soon became apparent as I "heard" the language of life speaking to me in some of the magazines that I reconnected with—*Psychology Today*, UTNE Reader, and my two new discoveries, ZOOMER and *Ki Awareness Magazine*—that I had to "decode" the message of life that I "heard" speaking to the modern world.

I've tried to explain what the language of life is in some of my musings, but it is such an elusive concept that I am almost compelled to approach it once more from a different angle just to bring all the clarity that I can muster to today's spiritual musing.

Everyone has had an AH-HA moment in his or her life, when a light goes on in our mind and we make an instant connection. "So that's what you meant!" one may shout, when it finally dawns on the husband who finally gets what his wife was trying to tell him (men can be very thick when it comes to women); or, someone working on a project that refused to come together until he had a dream that shifted his perspective and he saw the solution to his dilemma; or the writer who can't for the life of him figure out where to go next in his novel when out of the blue he gets an idea that dislodges him from his mental block.

These AH-HA moments are experiences in higher consciousness. We are raised to a level of awareness where we can "see" more clearly. This is what the language of life is—an AH-HA moment when we "see" or "hear" something that "speaks" to us in a silent voice, and we UNDERSTAND!

(Ascended Master St. Padre Pio did tell me in one spiritual healing session that life is all about GROWTH and UNDERSTANDING, and he shouted the words to my Spiritual Sensitive who was channeling him.)

The language of life can be "heard" and "seen," because the silent voice "speaks" to us in both sound and images. I have called the language of life "the omniscient guiding force of life," which was my reader-friendly way of describing how Divine Spirit helps Soul negotiate its way through life, or—as I used to like to say before I came to understand the subtle nuances of how karma works—keeps "old whore life" off our back!

I will expound upon the wiles of "old whore life" another time, but for now suffice to say that there is a shadowy side of life that everybody knows exists but few people want to acknowledge. But this is what writers are "called" to do—get to the truth of life!

"*Madame Bovary, c'est mois,*" said Gustave Flaubert when he was asked by his readers who his real life model was for the adulterous title character of his famous novel **Madame Bovary**. This suggests that "old whore life" is—well, this is what I intend to explore with this second edition of my spiritual musings...

So, what did the language of life say to me while I was sitting on the John yesterday?

When I heard the silent voice of the Way speaking the words **the way you do one thing is the way you do everything,** I heard a stern directive to be mindful of everything that I do, because how I do it reflects who I am. There was such powerful non-judgmental judgment in this directive that I felt like I was standing in front of the Lords of Karma as they stripped my life bare and revealed me for who I am!

If, as Alan Arkin said in his interview with Jian Ghomeshi on his show Q, "we are what we do," then it follows logically that how we do what we do determines what we are; but it feels like a quantum leap to say that **the way we do one thing is the way we do everything.** Is it a quantum leap, though?

Is the whole reflected in its parts? This is what this spiritual directive seems to be saying. Another way of expressing it would be: *everything we do reflects who we are.* That's the question, isn't it?

If this is true, then our life is an open book for those who have the gift of "reading" people. The historian Plutarch wrote a series of biographies of famous men to illuminate their common moral values and failings and compiled them into a book called *The Lives of Noble Greeks and Romans.*

As he studied the lives of these famous Greeks and Romans he cultivated his gift for "reading" people, and he made the extraordinary statement that "a simple gesture can reveal a great general's character as well as one of his greatest battle sieges."

Is it possible? Do we reveal our entire self through our simplest gesture? Is the whole contained in its parts?

Speaking for myself, I believe this is true. Perhaps this is why I have the gift of being able to see a whole book in one idea or insight. I call this "synoptic sight", being able to see the essential whole in its parts. This has happened with all of my books: I get a glimpse of the whole book, and then I have to work it out. Many artists have this gift.

Michael, the mystical teacher in Victor L. Wooten's novel *The Music Lesson,* said that everything already exists, and all we have to do is make it manifest through what we do—be it a song, a piece of music, a novel, a painting, or whatever; it's all there in the Great Universe of God just waiting to be made manifest. That was Michael's lesson to Victor.

So, if the part reflects the whole is it reasonable to say that *the way we do one thing is the way we do everything*?

Yes and no, because we are always free to change our ways.

I put my life under a microscope from the moment I "heard" those words sitting on the John, and it didn't take long to see that I am not as mindful of what I do as I would like to be, and I soon realized why I am a procrastinator—because I never really finish what I start. *And this shows in how I do what I do!*

So, yes; I agree that **the way we do one thing is the way we do everything,** and as we become mindful of what we do we soon see that how we do what we do reflects who we are; and I for one would like to change my habit of doing things the way I do, because on judgment day I don't want the Lords of Karma reading off a long list of everything that I left unfinished in my life!

What? I think I just heard something. The silent voice of the Way just spoke to me again. I think it's...**when you do something, do it right!**

4. The Magic Ingredient of Harmony

Friday, July 1, 2011 was Canada Day, and Penny and I drove to Canadian humorist Stephen Leacock's charming town of Orillia to enjoy our country's birthday celebration at Couchiching Beach Park, on the shores of downtown Orillia. I knew the parking lot would be full, so I parked our car in the old King's Buffet parking lot a few minutes' walk from the park. King's Buffet, where Penny and I often enjoyed a nice lunch, went out of business last summer, but the parking lot was almost full. We were lucky to find a spot.

We took our folding chairs out of the trunk and walked to the park, stopping by the public washrooms and sitting on the only empty bench for a break. A man with an aura of melancholy was sitting on one end of the bench, but we sat down anyway, and when Penny went to the washroom I struck up a conversation with the stranger; but I'll relate this experience in another musing that I've also been inspired to write, which I'm going to call "On Being a Keeper of the Flame."

Penny and I walked around the park checking out all the craft booths, and then we bought some fries and a soft drink and found a comfortable shady spot under the canopy of a huge maple tree in front of one of the band stands and parked our chairs and listened to a motley group playing blue grass as we ate our fries and sipped our cold drink.

I love people watching. In fact, watching the variety of people—old and young, tall and short, fat and thin, sporty and handicapped, different races, color, and religion, many sporting Canada Day T-shirts, hats, buttons, and little flags, all proud Canadians coming and going—inspired today's musing.

What set the idea free was the mixed-race family sitting in front of us in the shade of another huge maple tree—a tall, middle-aged Caucasian man and his Asian wife and two teenage children, the boy about twelve years old and the girl fifteen or sixteen, the man's octogenarian father, brother and wife and teenage daughter, all seated in folding chairs in a semi-circle having a picnic and listening to the music. I was surprised when my Muse whispered into my ear: "Connect the dots."

Nonplussed, I pondered for several minutes. "I should have brought my notebook," I said to Penny. "I've got an idea for a musing."

"Would you like me to go to the car and get it for you," she offered.

"Thank you sweetheart, but I think I can remember this idea."

"What's this musing about?" she asked.

"Connecting the dots," I said.

As curious as she was, Penny didn't pursue the subject. She knows not to interrupt the process when I'm in the grips of an idea, and I pondered on my musing until I caught the spirit of its meaning…

The creative mind thinks in images. When I saw the man put his arm around his Asian wife and look at her with such a loving smile on his face when they stood up to stretch their legs, I caught the first glimpse of the image that my Muse wanted me to see—an image of *harmony*.

I looked at their children. They were neither white nor Asian; they were a harmonious blend of the two races, and they had their own distinctive look, and I caught a deeper glimpse of *harmony*; and that's when I heard the silent voice, "Connect the dots."

We're free in this wonderful country; free to believe what we want, say what we think, love who we want, and pursue our dreams, and the only thing stopping us is ourselves. White, Asian, black, brown, yellow, it doesn't matter; Canada Day, proud, free, and open—one big family, I thought to myself—and that's when *harmony*, the idea for a spiritual musing popped into my mind!

I had already explored this idea in another musing in my book **Just Going With The Flow**, which I called "We're Only as Free as We Allow Ourselves to Be," but as I reflected on the idea of *harmony* I felt a tingling sensation, like I had just struck an exciting new musical note, and a warm feeling of goodness washed over me because I knew that my Muse wanted me to explore the music within…

Don't ask me what this means, but I know intuitively that this idea has to do with *harmony*, and as I reflected on this I saw why I felt the tingling sensation; it was like listening to a soft piece of classical music that soothes the aching heart, and *harmony* had to do with the blend of individual musical notes—the white husband's musical note with his Asian wife's musical note. In a word, their love for each other tuned them into the Sound of God, the Music of the Universe! *Wow!*

I couldn't help but think of **The Music Lesson: A Spiritual Search for Growth Through Music,** by Victor Wooten, and why my Muse wanted me to write a musing on the idea of *harmony*—because the omniscient guiding force of life wanted me to see that **love is the magic ingredient that brings everything into harmony,** a love that revealed itself to me as my mind processed all the information that I was taking in from all the people at Couchiching Park enjoying the Canada Day celebration!

"Music, like Life, and like you, is one entity expressing itself through its differences," said Michael, Victor Wooten's mystical music teacher. *"Music is one thing, but it wouldn't exist without its parts,"* he added, and that's how I felt about our wonderful country—one harmonious musical note made up of many separate notes!

But how did this come to be? How did multi-cultured Toronto become the model city of harmonious integration for the whole world?

Simple: Canada welcomed us. I was born in Calabria, Italy and my family was welcomed by Canada; and so have many families from other countries. We did not have to give up our language, culture, or beliefs to become Canadians; and this concept of freedom which lies at the very heart of democracy speaks to what Jesus called *"the wisdom of harmony, and the harmony of wisdom"*—the essential principal of his teaching!

"Love is who you are," said Jesus to Glenda Green, in her book **Love Without End, Jesus Speaks**; and as I reflected on my musing today I began to see why I was inspired by our Canada Day celebration to explore the music within—because by embracing the other, with all of his or her differences, as we have done in this country, we join in God's Orchestra and play in the symphony of love; and this is life at its best.

Thank you, Canada!

5. On Being a Keeper of the Flame

I wrote a whole book to explore how I became a Keeper of the Flame. I did not know what a Keeper of the Flame was until I explored this aspect of my life in my novel *Keeper of the Flame,* and now that I know what I am I'm having exciting little experiences that confirm my reality.

The first experience was the "coincidence" (I put coincidence in quotation marks, because I'm convinced Divine Spirit guides me to where I need to be) of coming to Victor L. Wooten's novel *The Music Lesson: A Spiritual Search For Growth Through Music.* Mary Hynes was interviewing Wooten on her radio show, CBC's *Tapestry,* and within minutes I knew that there was something special about "the greatest bass player in the world"; and I was right.

As he talked to Mary Hynes, I heard LOUD and CLEAR the Way being revealed by Victor Wooten, and I *knew* in my heart that he was a Keeper of the Flame who passed on the spiritual teachings of the Way through music; and I had to order his book to get the whole story.

I ordered *The Music Lesson* from Amazon.com, and to my surprise it arrived in four days (it usually takes a week) and I devoured the book in several readings, but when I came to the end of his book I was blown away by what Victor's mystical music teacher said to him on the penultimate page—"Remember, it is easy to play your instrument, but playing it well is not enough. It is time for you to enter the world of a true musician. It is time for you to become an ally of Music and share her blessing. You are now a keeper of the flame. Please keep that flame alive and do not, I say, *do not* allow Music to die."

There it was, in black and white—*Victor was a Keeper of the Flame! I couldn't believe my eyes!*

Victor was in training his whole life to become a Keeper of the Flame, and when Michael magically appeared in his apartment to give Victor the music lesson of his life Victor had no idea that he was being initiated into the invisible brotherhood of Keepers of the Flame—that secret order of people from all walks of life who keep the Holy Flame of God alive in the world; and when I read that Michael told Victor that he was now a Keeper of the Flame I had the confirmation I needed for my insight that there are as many entry points into the Way, which Jesus called the "kingdom of heaven," as there are souls. This is why Ascended Master St. Padre Pio told me that "life is a journey of the self."

Victor's entry point into the Way was music, and Michael taught him how to use music to enter the "kingdom of heaven," which simply means that Michael initiated Victor into the mysteries of life through music, and Victor was now spiritually obligated to pass on the Holy Flame of God to keep the Way of Music alive in the world.

The Music Lesson: A Spiritual Search for Growth Through Music was Victor L. Wooten's story of how he became a Keeper of the Flame, just as ***Keeper of the Flame*** was the story of how I became a Keeper of the Flame; and being a Keeper of the Flame I am also spiritually obligated to pass on the Holy Flame of God—which to my surprise I did twice last week; the first time at Couchiching Beach

Park in Orillia on Canada Day, and the next morning as I drove back to Orillia for a book discussion class on **Those Wonderful ECK Masters,** by Harold Klemp.

But I did not realize that I had passed on the Holy Flame of God on Friday afternoon to a retired toolmaker and Saturday morning to a couple of young hitchhikers on their way to British Columbia until a member of our book discussion class revealed something to me that puzzled all of us but finally gave up its meaning to me the following day.

Noreen (not her real name), who is a Spiritual Sensitive, not only saw two Spiritual Masters sitting beside me (Harold Klemp on my right and St. Padre Pio on my left), but she also saw a celestial harp just behind and above me, bathed in a golden light; but she could not tell me what that vision meant. I had to decode the message for myself.

"Oh no," I reacted when Noreen told me about the harp, *"don't tell me they're calling me home? I've got too much to do yet!"* By this I meant that I had more books to write before I crossed over.

"No, they just told me you're not going home yet," Noreen said, with a big grin on her face. "You have too much work to do."

What a relief! If I may then, let me relate the two surprising little experiences that I had of passing on the Holy Flame of God, which were later confirmed by Noreen's vision of the harp in golden light...

When Penny and I walked to the park Friday afternoon, I spotted an empty bench, the only one in that area, and I headed straight for it; but a man was walking in front of us, and he sat down on one end of the bench.

22

We sat down anyway, because Penny wanted to use the public washroom; and while I waited for her I struck up a conversation with the stranger. "Isn't it a gorgeous day for Canada Day?" I said.

Surprised to be addressed, the man said, "It sure is."

The waterfront was full with cabin cruises and sailboats of all sizes, and the boardwalk was crowded with people walking to and fro. "Are you from Orillia?" I asked the stranger.

He replied yes, and this gave me the entry point that I needed to open up our conversation because Stephen Leacock, one of my favorite writers, retired in Orillia (which he called Mariposa in his humorous book of stories *Sunshine Sketches of a Little Town*) after teaching political economics at McGill University in Montreal for years, and I informed him that I was a writer also, and this excited the man's curiosity and opened the spigot for the "water of everlasting life" (the Way) to pour out of me and quench the stranger's thirst for the spiritual inspiration that his soul cried for.

I had no idea that he needed to be touched by the Holy Flame of God, but I did sense his loneliness and spiritual ennui. He wasn't part of the Canada Day crowd, and I picked up on his apartness; that's why I was nudged to strike up a conversation with him, and within minutes he informed me that he had thought of writing some stories on his own life.

I encouraged him with enthusiasm, telling the retired toolmaker about the memoir I had just finished reading **(Sidney Poitier, *Life Beyond Measure:* Letters to My Great Granddaughter),** and what a wonderful legacy it would be to pass on his life story to his children and grandchildren the way the trailblazing Hollywood black actor did to his great-granddaughter Ayele LaBarrie.

We talked some more, about how to write his own book of stories and how to get it published on the Internet, the satisfaction that comes with the creative process, how it gives you something to look forward to each day, and by the time Penny returned the Holy Flame of God had put a light into the stranger's eyes, and he thanked me for sharing what I did, telling me that he was going to look into writing his own life stories.

"You should. It's a great legacy to pass on to your kids," I said, not really knowing if he had any children or grandchildren; but he didn't correct me, so he must have had a family.

And that's how we parted, with him smiling in surprised wonder at the idea of writing his own stories, something like Leacock but more in the vein of Sidney Poitier whom he loved as an actor as much as I did; and the second incident of passing on the Holy Flame of God happened the following morning, and it also had to do with writing…

It's about an hour's drive to Orillia from Tiny Beaches where Penny and I live, and I decided to take Highway 12 instead of the Horseshoe Valley Road because I wanted to stop at Tim Hortons in Midland and pick up a coffee for my drive.

I was going to my monthly book discussion class. I passed two young hitchhikers on the outskirts of Midland and pulled over. I had my Saturday *Globe and Mail* paper that I had just picked up in Wyevale on the passenger's seat, as well as a copy of the book that we were studying, and on my back seat I had six copies of my novel **Keeper of the Flame** still wrapped in clear plastic in packages of two, and some other stuff that had to be moved over to one side for one of the hitchhikers to sit.

The young man opened the passenger's door and I told him I was going to Orillia. "We just want a ride to the 400 cutoff," he replied.

"I can take you right to it," I said.

"Great. Can we put our stuff in the back, or—?"

"Yeah, just put it in the back seat," I replied.

The young lady—they were in their early twenties—opened the door and placed her knapsack in the back seat and she then placed his on top of hers. I picked up the newspaper and book from the front seat and said, "You can hold these in your lap till we get there. It's not far."

"Sure," he said, and when they were comfortably seated I pulled out and thus began my second experience of passing on the Holy Flame of God, inspired by the conversation that I struck with the young man; but it was curious how it came about, because it happened so naturally.

The young man, who introduced himself as Pat, studied the book he was holding and then asked me if I lived in Orillia.

"No, I live in Tiny Beaches. I'm going to Orillia for a book discussion class on that book you have in your hands."

"Oh," he said, and looked at it again.

"Actually, I'm a writer also," I said, surprising myself, and then turned and asked the young lady to hand me one of the packages of my novel. "It's on the seat under your knapsacks." She found it and handed it to me. I gave it to Pat. "I just got this one published last month," I added.

"Wow. You're a writer? Congratulations," Pat said.

"Pat writes too," the young lady said excitedly. "He's a poet."

"No kidding? Good for you, Pat. I love poetry. Poetry is one of the best ways to initiate yourself into the mysteries of life," I said, feeling a powerful surge of energy wash over me as it always does whenever I'm about to connect with another Soul in that special way (just as I did with the stranger at the park in Orillia the day before).

"I like to write poetry," Pat said proudly, and then stared at the eye-catching image of the Flaming Heart on the cover of my book again, and then he turned the package of two books over and started reading the back cover. "Pilgrim's Progress?" he said, his curiosity excited. The first line of my synopsis got his attention: "***Keeper of the Flame*** is a modern day Pilgrim's Progress," but rather than finish reading the synopsis, he asked, "What's it about?"

"It was inspired by my past-life regressions," I answered, and by the blank stare I got I had to ask, "Do you know what a past-life regression is?"

"No. I never heard of it," he said.

"What's your spiritual background?" I asked.

"I'm a Roman Catholic," he said.

"Okay," I said, with an ironic smile. "I was a Roman Catholic too, but I had to move on in my search. "Have you heard of reincarnation?"

"No," he said, with another blank stare.

"You haven't? In this day and age? *Good God, Pat! And you want to be a poet?* A poet has to be aware of the world around him. Check out Jack Kerouac. He wrote the famous novel ***On the Road*** based on his trip across the states with his friend Neal Cassady—"

"Yeah, we read *On the Road,*" the young lady jumped in.

"There you go, then," I said.

"He also wrote a book called ***Dharma Bums***," Pat offered.

"Yes he did. Kerouac was also a poet, and ***Dharma Bums*** was inspired by his poet friend Gary Snyder. I don't care for Kerouac's writing, but I love Snyder's poetry. My favorite is *What Have I Learned.* 'When you get it right, you pass it on,' he said. I love that line. Did you know that Jack Kerouac was a Roman Catholic who became a Buddhist? He knew about reincarnation. Reincarnation is the belief that we have lived before in another life. My novel ***Keeper of the Flame*** is the story of how my past lives affected my current life..."

And that's how the young poet and his companion were introduced to the Holy Flame of God, and before I let them off at the 400 North to Parry Sound ramp, I was "compelled" to give him a cram course on the art of writing poetry, using the poet Adrienne Rich's definition of poetry as my entry point into the mysteries of life ("**poetry is an act of the imagination transforming reality into a deeper perception of what is**") which, if the young man fans the Holy Flame of God, will initiate him into the mysteries of life with the Way of Poetry just as Victor Wooten was initiated with the Way of Music and Gurdjieff's teaching of "work on oneself" had initiated me; but I did not know that I had passed on the Holy Flame of God to the young poet and his companion until Noreen saw the vision of the harp bathed in a golden light at our book discussion class!

It came as a joyful revelation. I knew that Noreen's vision was telling me something symbolically, but it didn't hit me until the following day when I made the connection with my last spiritual musing in **Just Going with the Flow,** called "Being the Music."

The harp symbolized my life as a Keeper of the Flame. I played in the Orchestra of God with the "music" of my own life!

I'm a writer, and creative writing is my "harp." And the stranger at the park in Orillia got to "hear" my "music" (the individual sound of the Way that Keepers of the Flame play in the Orchestra of God), and the young poet that I picked up Saturday morning also got to "hear" my "music"; and I was so excited that I had to call Noreen and explain the meaning of her vision!

She agreed with my interpretation, and then she told me something that I didn't expect: "You're going to meet that man again."

"Who, the man in the park?"

"Yes," she said.

"That should be interesting, because I never gave him my name and he didn't give me his. Are you sure, Noreen?"

"That's what I was told," she said.

"Wow. I can't wait," I said.

After our chat I had to go for a long walk to level off my energies; but they were so high from my two experiences of passing on the Holy Flame of God that it took a good week to settle down.

6. I Saw Old Whore Life the Other Day

I saw "old whore life" the other day. She came out to frustrate Charlie, a contractor that I know and work for occasionally. When I returned the key to the owner of the cottage I had just finished painting in Tiny Beaches, he asked if I could do him a favor. "Do you know any plumbers?" he asked. "I have to change a toilet."

I couldn't think of anyone offhand, but then Charlie came to mind. Charlie wasn't licensed, but he often did plumbing and electrical work on his renovation jobs. I had done drywall taping and painting for him on a few jobs, and I knew he was very handy. "I know someone. In fact, I have his card in my van," I said.

My customer lived in Toronto, and he would have to drive up to show Charlie what he wanted done, and then he would have to drive back up to pay him; that's why he asked if I could take care of it for him.

I couldn't say no. My customer had been good to me. He had given me over three thousand dollars worth of work. Besides, it was nice to push some work Charlie's way. Charlie had been good to me also.

"Okay," I said. "Show me what you want done."

We went inside and he showed me the toilet he wanted changed. It was the original toilet, thirty years old; but it had started to plug up and he had to snake it a couple of times and decided it was time for a new one; but I couldn't promise him when Charlie could do it.

My customer said he was coming back the following Saturday, so if Charlie could do it by then he could pay him.

"I'll call Charlie and find out when he can do it. He called me last week (Charlie always calls me when he's had a few beers and needs to dump on somebody) and he told me he was swamped with work, so I don't know when he can fit you in."

"Call him. If he can do it by next Saturday I can pay him. Cash. You keep the key. Can you do this for me?"

"Okay," I said. "You want a regular toilet?"

"Yeah. Nothing fancy."

That night I called Charlie, but he couldn't promise he could get to it by Saturday, but he would try. "Does he want me to pick up a new toilet?"

"If you would. Get a low end, not too expensive; but maybe you should drive down to see what you have to do. Come to my place and I can take you there."

Charlie lives in Wasaga Beach, and it was a fifteen-minute drive to Tiny Beaches. "Why drive down twice? I'll pick up the toilet. I think I can do it Friday morning. You going to be home?"

"Yeah," I said, but Charlie called the next day to tell me he could do it Thursday morning instead. Some tiles for another job hadn't come in yet, so he was free Thursday. He drove down to my house and followed me to the cottage. He had another man with him.

I showed him the toilet and immediately Charlie went into work mode, a focused attitude that brooked no nonsense. It was so far from his off-work personality that I smiled whenever I saw this change in him.

There was a wire rack with towels screwed to the wall behind the toilet, so he asked his helper to get a star screwdriver out of the truck while he inspected what he had to do.

"Oh shit. He's got a copper line. I didn't bring my soldering kit," he said, as I took the towels off the rack and placed them into the tub.

"I told you to come down and look at it," I said.

"I should've," he said. "I have to go back to the Beach. I need a new shut-off valve too. This one's too high. Shit. We have to shut off the water. Where's the waterline shut-off?"

"He didn't tell me. He didn't think you had to shut off the waterline."

"I have to shut the water off to change this line. Shit," he said, and we had to hunt around for the trap door to the crawl space of the cottage; but there was no trap door because there was no crawl space.

We went outside to look. There was a lid to a small space under the cottage that held the hot water tank, and within minutes Charlie found the water shut-off valve.

Back in the washroom, Charlie flushed the toilet to empty the tank and his helper got the top two screws off, but the rack wouldn't lift off; it had a bar that was in behind the copper line and the rack was too close to the outside wall to unscrew the bar.

"Just leave it. Let me get the toilet out first," Charlie said, but when he started wrenching the nut off the whole bolt rotated. "Shit. It's all rusted. This thing's ancient. Okay, this means war. Go get me my hacksaw."

Charlie's tone changed. The "old whore" had tried his patience, and it was time to do battle. His helper brought the hacksaw and Charlie went to work. He hacked off one bolt, and while still breathing heavy he attacked the second bolt and didn't stop until he cut through. "That should do it," he said, panting as he tried to lift the toilet off; but it was awkward in the tight space, and his helper had to give him a hand.

One morning over breakfast with Charlie before we went to the house he was renovating (I was taping the new drywall), he said something that I never forgot because it cut to the quick: *"All we're allowed is survival."*

We were talking about how hard it was to get ahead when you're self-employed like we were. Just when you think you've made some progress, something comes up to set you back. "That's old whore life, Charlie," I said. "She won't let you get ahead. She'll do everything she can to screw you. It takes a lot of determination to get ahead of the game."

"That's for damn sure," Charlie said.

They took the old toilet out of the cottage and placed it on the front lawn and dumped out the rest of the water in the bowl and then put it into the back of the truck to haul off to the dump.

Charlie took the new toilet out of the box and they brought it into the cottage. "I have to go to the Beach and get a new shut-off valve and a fitting for the copper pipe. I won't be long," he said.

"Here," I said, and gave him the key. "I'll go home. Call when you're done."

Two hours later Charlie called. "All done."

"Good. Everything okay?" I asked.

"Yeah. No leaks. Everything's fine," he said.

"Alright, I'll be right there," I said, and in a few minutes I pulled into the driveway. They were outside. Charlie crushed his cigarette butt under his foot and went into his truck to write out his bill. My customer didn't want to pay more than five hundred dollars for the whole job, but Charlie's bill was under three, which included the price of the new toilet. "What about travel? Did you charge for that?" I asked.

"Ten bucks for gas," he said.

"No way. Twenty bucks a trip. Two trips, forty bucks," I said.

"That's too much," he said.

"Bullshit. You've given him a great price; the least you can do is get a little travel money out of it. Forty bucks, Charlie."

He added the forty dollars, which brought his bill to three hundred and twenty-five dollars, and my customer couldn't believe it when he drove up Saturday to pay me for Charlie's work; he was used to Toronto prices, and he gave me a hundred dollars for my inconvenience, and a special bottle of wine imported from Italy for my painting job.

"You know what, sweetheart," I said to Penny later over a glass of wine on our deck before dinner, "good people are generous people."

"Yes, they are," she agreed.

"And conversely—" I said, and broke into laughter; but "old whore life" hadn't finished with Charlie yet.

I called him Monday morning to meet for coffee and pay him for his work, but he was too busy. "I can drop by your house around three," he said.

"Good. I'll have a cold one waiting for you," I said; but when Charlie dropped by later he couldn't stay. He had to pick up his men, who didn't have a vehicle. When I handed him the money, he said, "I didn't make much today.

I got pulled over for running a stop sign this afternoon. It cost me a hundred and twenty bucks. You just can't win."

7. A Message from Groundhog

"Life is a journey of the self," said Ascended Master St. Padre Pio; but where did the self come from? And where is it going?

I explored these questions in my novel *Keeper of the Flame*, and I came to the understanding that the self comes from God. "Trailing clouds of glory do we come /From God who is our home," said Wordsworth.

So our journey through life is a journey back to our spiritual home, the Body of God, the Ocean of Love and Mercy; but herein lies the mystery, because making sense of this journey can be confusing, one person calling it "a tale told by an idiot full of sound and fury signifying nothing," and another calling it "a journey of the alone to the Alone." This is why I'm writing these musings. I want to make sense of our journey through life…

Life is hard, cruel, and unforgiving, and it can reduce a grown man to say, "All we're allowed is survival." If this is true, who or what is it that only allows us survival? Is it "old whore life"? Does "old whore life" have that much power over us? William Ernest Henley, the poet who wrote *Invictus*, didn't think so:

> Out of the night that covers me,
>   Black as the Pit from pole to pole,
> I thank whatever gods may be
>   For my unconquerable soul.
> In the fell clutch of circumstance

I have not winced nor cried aloud.
Under the bludgeonings of chance
My head is bloody, but unbowed.

Beyond this place of wrath and tears
    Looms but the horror of the shade,
And yet the menace of the years
    Finds, and shall find me, unafraid.

It matters not how straight the gate,
    How charged with punishments the scroll,
I am the master of my fate:
I am the captain of my soul.

Henley saw "old whore life" with his poet's discerning eye—"the bludgeonings of chance"—but he refused to submit to the "old whore." He continued to charge at life, his "head bloody, but unbowed."

But why bother, one asks? Why must one keep charging at life when there seems to be no end to the "bludgeonings of chance"? It doesn't matter how hard we try, we all know that "old whore life"—"the menace of the years"—won't stop screwing us of our virtue!

And yet, regardless "how straight the gate, /How charged with punishment the scroll," we have such longing in our soul to return back home to God that we will find our way out of "the fell clutch of circumstance" and become masters of our fate and captains of our soul...

Imagine if you will, a ship lost at sea, blown hither and thither by the trade winds because it has no captain to steer its course. Now let this ship be man's soul, blown hither and thither by the capricious winds of life because it has no captain to steer its course; how long will it take for this ship to find its way back home to the Port of God? Forever.

"One generation passeth away, and another generation cometh, but the earth abideth forever," said the Preacher in Ecclesiastes. So let us imagine the unimaginable and believe that we can take charge of our own life and steer our ship wherever we desire, and further imagine messengers sent from God to help guide our ship, a bird for example, or a dolphin that appears out of the blue to guide us through the dangerous waters and shoals of life. Would we be asking too much of God? No. And I'd like to share with you how some of God's messengers have guided me...

The most recent messenger was a groundhog that came to our house several days after the spiritual experience I had at my book discussion class in Orillia last Saturday that confirmed I am a Keeper of the Flame; but I will relate this experience last. Let me begin with an experience that I had with a turtle a few years ago when I was still living in Northwestern Ontario.

Divine Spirit, the omniscient guiding force of life, often speaks to us through the animal kingdom. For centuries people have been reading the signs of birds and animals to guide their way. In the old days these people who read the language of life were called soothsayers, seers, and shamans; but anyone can read the signs and symbols if they are open to the language of life.

A word, if I may, about the language of life. As mystical as this may sound, it is as common as the weather—because it is life itself. It's a big concept to get one's head around, but life itself is the Way, and by Way I mean the specific consciousness of the spiritual direction home to God.

To use the metaphor of the captain steering his ship home to the Port of God, let the Way be the specific course that Divine Spirit gives to the captain to sail his ship back to Port; but bear in mind that the captain has to steer his course through the many vicissitudes of life, so the specific course that Spirit gives to the captain will change according to the circumstances, and it is forever changing course but always set home to the Port of God.

For example, I was driving home from Winnipeg where I visited my sister a few years ago when I saw a turtle in the middle of the highway just as I was approaching the Ontario border. I pulled over and picked the little turtle up and placed him on the side of the road. "There," I said, "now you're safe," and I got back into my new little sports car and sped off.

To my surprise, I got pulled over for speeding a few minutes after I crossed over into Ontario. I got a speeding ticket and lost points on my driver's license; but I never realized that Divine Spirit had sent me a sign in the turtle to slow down. *Divine Spirit was looking after me, but I wasn't listening!*

Did "old whore life" give me the speeding ticket? That's the question, isn't it?

But I learned my lesson. Once I connected the dots and realized that the turtle had been sent by Divine Spirit to give me a sign to slow down so I wouldn't be frustrated by "old whore life," I paid a little more attention to the signs, and it paid off a year or so later when I was driving to a job in Longlac.

I don't know if I was speeding or not, but when I saw a mother duck crossing the highway with five or six little ducklings I slowed down. "I'll bet there's a radar trap ahead," I thought to myself. And sure enough, I spotted an OPP cruiser parked in a side road with his radar gun sticking out the window; but thanks to the ducks, I wasn't speeding.

One can dismiss this as a mere coincidence, but I don't. I know that the omniscient guiding force of life gave me a warning sign to watch my speed, and I paid attention and spared myself the grief. But I got caught by the "old whore" a couple of months ago in Wasaga Beach when I failed to come to a full stop at a stop sign. Penny has told me many times to come to a complete stop, but I never listened; and finally my "kissing-stop karma" caught up to me and the "old whore" screwed me of a hundred and ten dollars!

"Kissing-stop karma" and "old whore life"—does it begin to make sense now? That's what these spiritual musings are all about...

I had another memorable experience with a sign from the bird kingdom that inspired my short story "The Turkey Vulture" when I was still living in Northwestern Ontario. It happened at the town cemetery.

I was a pallbearer for my friend's funeral. He was a heavy equipment contractor who passed away shortly after his wife. He had dreamt his whole life of becoming a millionaire, and shortly before he passed he told me that he had finally "made it." But he had no children to leave it to.

He had four siblings, three sisters and one brother. His brother worked for him most of his life, but when my friend died he didn't live up to his promise of "taking care" of his brother.

So there we were at the cemetery when I spotted a strange looking bird up in a tree. "What kind of bird is that?" I asked the man standing beside me, a heavy equipment contractor from Thunder Bay who had come to my friend's funeral out of respect for a fellow contractor.

"I think it's a turkey vulture," he said.

"Turkey vulture? I've never seen any in this area before," I said.

"That's what it looks like to me," he said.

"A turkey vulture?" I repeated, and suddenly broke into laughter. "Wow," I said. "That's a sign. The vultures are going to come out of the woodwork now. It's going to be fun when they read that will—"

And fun it was. The "old whore" caused such infighting that it took several years and a lot of legal expenses to settle my friend's estate, which caused such animosity among the siblings that some stopped speaking to each other. In fact, my friend's brother went to his grave never forgiving his brother for not being true to his word…

Signs and symbols. They're everywhere. Last Wednesday I saw a groundhog in our back yard. He was grazing on the clover in our lawn in front of our back shed. We have our bird feeder there, and a block of oak that I use to chop kindling for our airtight woodstove. When I feed "the critters," as Penny calls our little family of chipmunks, squirrels, blue jays, and crows that come daily for their share of peanuts and bird seeds, I spread the food around so they can all get some, so I put peanuts and seeds on the block of oak as well as the feeder and on top of my woodpile—because if I put the food in only one place it brings out the aggressive survival instinct in the critters, which is not a pleasant sight to watch.

The groundhog was an anomaly. We've had raccoons and skunks come around for food, but seldom groundhogs. Only once a few years ago did we see a groundhog in our backyard, but we didn't have our book **ANIMAL SPIRIT GUIDES** then, so we didn't know that the groundhog had come to bring us a message.

"When something out of the ordinary happens, it means that Spirit is trying to tell you something," someone once said (I think it was Harold Klemp), and the groundhog was an anomaly; so I took out our **ANIMAL SPIRIT GUIDES** book by Steven D. Farmer, Ph.D., and read what Groundhog (the collective spirit of groundhogs) had to say:

"If Groundhog shows up, it means: You're about to investigate a new area of study that will require intensive effort on your part, but will be well worth it. Pay close attention to your dreams at this time and see if you can discern their meaning. You're going through an initiation, one where you'll experience a cycle of death-rebirth, and emerge with a new sense of self. As you experiment with altered states of consciousness, you'll find your experiences become more intense and stronger. Communicate your boundaries and limits clearly and straightforwardly" (p. 167).

In light of what I had experienced on Saturday at our book discussion class on Spiritual Masters, several days before the groundhog showed up in our backyard, Farmer's explanation of Groundhog's message made sense to me. Not only did the cute little groundhog show up and graze in our backyard, but he also poised himself on my chopping block and stared at our kitchen window for several hours—as if to say to me, "I'm here to tell you something you need to know."

I had no idea what message Groundhog had come to give me, but after I read Farmer's explanation it all fell into place: It was an extraordinary spiritual class. Not only did Noreen see two Spiritual Masters sitting beside me as well as the celestial harp bathed in a golden light right behind and just above me, but I also had a remarkable experience when we did the visualization technique that Joan guided us through.

We were to imagine walking a beautiful ocean beach, feeling the breeze and sand and water splashing on our feet, and as we walked we were to image the Spiritual Master we were studying that day walking down the beach to meet us. When we met, we could ask him anything we wanted and pay close attention to what he had to say.

The Spiritual Master that we were studying that day is one of my favorite Masters, and the moment we met on the beach I said to him: "Before you say anything, I want to thank you for everything you have done for me. I am eternally grateful for your guidance."

He didn't say a word. In my mind's eye, I saw him holding a flaming torch in his left hand, but he brought his arm down and the torch changed into a flaming heart, which he held in the palm of his hands, and he stretched out his hands and passed the flaming heart into my cupped hands.

The flaming heart looked exactly like the flaming heart image on the cover of my book *Keeper of the Flame*. The Spiritual Master still did not say a word. He didn't have to. I understood what he had done. He had just validated that I was a Keeper of the Flame!

This was such a powerful experience that for several days, right up to the day Groundhog came to give me a message, I felt like the atoms of my being were being rearranged. I said to Penny, "I feel like my psyche has been scrambled. I've never felt anything like this in my life!"

I didn't know what was happening to me. And then Groundhog came to validate my initiation. When the Spiritual Master passed on the flaming heart he confirmed my initiation into the secret brotherhood of the Keepers of the Flame. Once I made the connection, the groundhog left; and we haven't seen him since.

8. Life Is a Never-ending Rite of Passage

It seems to me that life is a never-ending rite of passage, from one state of consciousness to another without end. Perhaps that's why they say that the only constant in life is change. But change from what to what?

Consciousness. From one state, presumably lower, to a higher state of consciousness until, ultimately, one realizes what the mystics have been talking about for centuries—divine-realization consciousness.

But what if one doesn't believe in God? Where does all of that life force bursting for expression go? Work? Love? Sex? Science? Philanthropy? Life, life, and more life!

Godless people are passionate people, not because their life force is spent denying their inherent drive to divine-realization consciousness, but because their life force is poured into a mental paradigm that cannot possibly contain the conatus of God, and it spills over into monumental works of literature, art, music, architecture, social causes, or whatever.

Not to say that God believers are not passionate. On the contrary, the greater one's belief in God the more passionate one's life becomes, because one is forever trying to fill the immortal archetypal self of his life which can never be filled. It is a conundrum!

I was born into the latter category, which is why I became a seeker at such an early age; and I could not pour myself into myself fast enough. I was always seeking, seeking, seeking—pouring, pouring, pouring myself into a self without limits...

I discovered a new writer yesterday, T. Coraghessan Boyle, a brilliant novelist and short story writer who scares the literature out of me! Again, like so many other books that I have discovered, I found his novel *The Women* by "chance" yesterday.

I drove into Barrie yesterday morning to have coffee and chat with my friend at her bookstore, but she had taken the day off; so I drove to Bayfield Mall to browse. I found myself at the same discount book fair where I "chanced" upon two books that I needed for research on my novel *Healing with Padre Pio*—John Updike's novel *Seek My Face* (a metaphor for man's inherent drive for divine realization consciousness), and *90 Minutes in Heaven* (a true story of confirmation of life after death), by Don Piper. Yesterday my eye was pulled to TC Boyle's novel, and the moment I started reading the jacket I felt such gravitational attraction for this writer that I *had* to explore him!

I also bought two other books that caught my eye: *The Garden of Truth,* a book on Sufism by Sayyed Hossein Nasr, and *The Best American Spiritual Writing,* edited by Phillip Zaleski; and I left the mall with a feeling that this was the reason I was nudged to drive into Barrie—which was confirmed when I got home and began reading Boyle's novel!

A new personal aphorism sprang to mind this morning as I tried to explain to Penny why Boyle scares the literature out of me—***"the better you get at what you do, the more you are attracted to the best,"*** and by this I simply mean that everything I feel I have learned about writing was blown away like dust in a sandstorm! TC Boyle is a master of his craft, a brilliant storyteller, and reading him fills me with such love and admiration for the craft that I want to—*I have to!*—perfect my own style and dance to the tune of my own "music" the way Boyle dances to his!

My God, what literary music! I had to go on the Internet and research TC Boyle, and—not to my surprise, because I knew in the depths of my soul that he was concentrating his life force into a scintillating genius that defined his satirical voice—I learned that he belonged to the category of the Godless people; that's why his writing has a depth of passion that makes my head swoon with sheer aesthetic pleasure!

I could envy him, he's such a brilliant writer; but I don't, and I will learn from him because he is one of the best of the best. And yet...

But why did I have the feeling that he belonged to the category of Godless people after only reading three chapters of *The Women*—a novel based upon the famous American architect Frank Lloyd Wright whose fourth wife Olgivanna Milanoff was a student of the same Russian mystic whom I had studied for years, George Ivanovitch Gurdjieff?

I "heard" Boyle's voice as I read *The Women*. Something about the author's voice alerted me to his personal paradigm, and by this I mean his central motif, or philosophy of life—which focused on the human condition with such concentration that I sensed this was all there was for TC Boyle—meaning, he was one of the Godless people.

"Life is tragic and absurd and none of it has any purpose at all," TC Boyle reveals in an interview with

Richard Grant (The Guardian, *Saturday 28, February 2009*). "Science has killed religion, there's no hope for the future with seven billion of us on the planet, and the only thing you can do is laugh in the face of it all," he amplified; and his laughter at life comes through in his garrulous, satirical voice.

I addressed the question of the absurdity of life in my spiritual musing "Life Is Not Meaningless And Absurd" in my first book of spiritual musings *Just Going With The Flow*, so I need not repeat myself; but I am compelled to address the issue of the limited personal paradigm that holds back the life force like a dam holding back the river of life and flooding social consciousness with such passionate intensity that it inhibits man's natural impulse for divine realization consciousness.

"He can write," said the critic Bill Seligman about TC Boyle, "and he can imagine with more energy than any of his contemporaries. But energy is not enough; there's only so far you can go on sheer technique. And until he goes further, he'll remain a satirist cut off from the oxygen of morality." But sadly, this brilliant writer can't go any further as long as he clings to his "stone" of unbelief.

In one of my spiritual healing sessions with my Medical Intuitive for my book *Healing with Padre Pio*, Ascended Master St. Padre Pio said that "we create our own suffering with our beliefs," and he illustrated this with the image of a person placing a large stone in the River of Life that impeded the flow of the water.

The stone symbolizes one's beliefs that impede the flow of the life force in one's life. Jesus called the life force the "water of everlasting life," and his teaching was all about letting the "water of everlasting life" flow in one's life. In short, Jesus taught us how to realize our divine nature.

I had a big "stone" that impeded the flow of my life force, that's why I went for a spiritual healing with my Medical Intuitive who was assisted by St. Padre Pio; and, I'm happy to say, the Good Saint's humility devastated my vanity and removed my big "stone," and the "water of everlasting life" flows much more freely in my life now.

My spiritual healing sessions with St. Padre Pio were a rite of passage for me, a passage from vanity to humility; and when the Spiritual Master Rebazar Tarzs handed me the Flaming Heart during our visualization technique at our spiritual book discussion class a couple of weeks ago, I experienced another rite of passage and was officially accepted into the brotherhood of Keepers of the Flame. And, as I came to realize with my unexpected experience with TC Boyle's writing, I find myself going through another rite of passage, but this passage is my initiation into the privileged order of creative writers.

In his book *The Rites of Passage,* Arnold Van Gennep says that rites of passage have three phases. In the first phase, people withdraw from their current status and prepare to move from one place or status to another. There is often a detachment or "cutting away" from the former self in this phase. The second phase is a transition, a period between states, during which one has left one place or state but hasn't yet entered or joined the next. And in the third, re-incorporation phase, the passage is consummated and one is now realized in his new state of consciousness—until his next rite of passage, that is, because life is a never-ending rite of passage.

I wrote my novel *Keeper of the Flame* to creatively explore how I initiated myself into the secret brotherhood of Keepers of the Flame, which was officially confirmed in a vision when Rebazar Tarzs handed me the Holy Flame of God one month after *Keeper of the Flame* was published, but I had no idea that I was also going through a rite of passage into the brotherhood of creative writers until TC Boyle set me ablaze with a new imperative to improve the quality of my writing! And if one may think that this is the product of a fanciful imagination, let me throw another surprising little experience into the mix just to sweeten this spiritual musing...

In *Rites of Passage*, Gennep concluded that having completed the rite and assumed their "new" identity, one re-enters society with one's new status. Re-incorporation is characterized by elaborate rituals and ceremonies, like debutant balls and college graduation, and by new ties signs: thus "in rites of incorporation (the third phase of the rite of passage) there is a widespread use of the 'sacred bond,' the "sacred chord, the knot, and of analogous forms such as the *belt* (italics mine), the ring, the bracelet and the crown."

When I went to the Bayfield Mall to browse the day I "discovered" TC Boyle, I walked past a store that had merchandise displayed in the walkway for passing customers. My eye instantly fell upon a rack of belts with a sale price: 1 for $5, 2 for $9.

I needed a new belt, and several times while shopping in Wal-Mart the past few months I tried on a new belt, but I never purchased one; this time I felt compelled to buy not one, but two belts!

I continued browsing, and then found myself at the book fair where my eye fell upon TC Boyle's novel *The Women*, which I bought; and I continued to browse the book shelves until I came upon *The Garden of Truth*, which spoke to my initiation into the secret brotherhood ("*I, you, he, she, we, /In the garden of mystic lovers, /these are not true distinctions,*" said Rumi in a poem that confirmed my quest for God), and I also bought *The Best American Spiritual Writing* for pleasure reading.

How in God's name would I know that a belt symbolized the "sacred bond" of the incorporation phase of the rite of passage? I didn't know this until I began writing this musing and did some research on rites of passage on the Internet!

So there you have it, the two belts that I purchased were symbolic confirmation of my rite of passage into the brotherhood of Keepers of the Flame and the privileged order of creative writers, which confirmed for me that life is an never-ending rite of passage from one state of consciousness to another!

9. Doing for Others

There are many ways to keep "old whore life" off your back, but one of the best ways is doing for others…

That's today's spiritual musing. That thought came to me the other day when Penny shared her workday with me on our front deck when she got home around four. I put the novel I was reading down (it was difficult to put down **The Women**, by my new literary discovery TC Boyle) and got Penny a glass of wine.

"I had an interesting experience today," she told me after a few sips, and she related her experience with an elderly man who asked if she could help him find a beach ball.

Penny is a Hallmark representative, and she was doing her work in the card section of the Wal-Mart store in Wasaga Beach. "I'm sorry, sir," she said to the man who had wheeled up to her in a motorized shopping cart, "but I don't work for Wal-Mart. But I did see some beach balls in Action Alley."

Action Alley is an aisle that Wal-Mart sets up for discount sales.

The man thanked her and scooted off. He returned a few minutes later and told Penny there were no beach balls in Action Alley. "If you go to Customer's Service, they can page someone to help you," she said to the elderly gentleman, and he thanked her again and scooted off.

Seven or eight minutes later he returned and in a plaintive voice said to Penny, "They weren't any help. They told me to look in one of the aisles. They should be there, the lady said; but I couldn't find any."

"This time I did what I should have done in the first place," Penny said, and said to the man, "Come on. Let's go see if we can find you a beach ball," and she put her workbag under one of the card bins and went with the frustrated gentleman to find his beach ball.

They found one, and then Penny went back to the card department to finish her work and the gentleman continued shopping.

About twenty minutes later, his shopping all done, he scooted back to the card department and thanked Penny again for all her help. He was very appreciative.

"I have no idea why he wanted a beach ball," Penny said, "but it wasn't a big thing. It wasn't like I had to go way out of my way or anything, but it meant a lot to the old fellow."

I smiled at Penny's generous spirit. "It may not seem like much, but *doing for others is one of the best ways to keep 'old whore life' off your back,*" I said, and broke into laughter at my new saying.

Penny joined in my laughter, but by sheer "coincidence"—and once again, I put the word in quotation marks because I know that Divine Spirit was working another idea for a spiritual musing!—I happened to catch CBC's *Tapestry*, hosted by Mary Hynes a couple of hours before Penny came home, and it also had to do with the spiritual concept of *doing for others...*

The *Sunday, July 10, 2011* edition of *Tapestry* was called "Baby Guru." Mary Hynes spoke with psychologist and philosopher Alison Gopnik (*The Philosophical Baby*), who argues that babies might have more to teach us than we realize. Also, Hynes featured a documentary by CBC producer Frank Faulk, who introduces us to Gary Davis, a happily married man and father of two grown children. He also has a successful career in business, and he had a very interesting story to tell us.

One might think that Gary Davis has it all figured out, but Gary tells us that he has nothing figured out, and that's okay. The people who taught him his life lessons hadn't figured it out either. Gary's teachers weren't professors, gurus or psychologists; they were the babies he met as a young man working at a daycare center and the terminally ill patients he sits with now when he volunteers at the Queensway-Carlton Hospital in Ottawa.

Gary's story is about **doing for others,** but what fascinated me about his story is the trajectory of his life—from an inquisitive child who asked his mother at the age of six the big question about life ("what are we here for?"), to the college student who had an intimate experience with a young lady that threw him into a panic because it forced him to see that he was a stranger to himself, to the young man who worked for a daycare center and whose love for children opened his heart and reconnected him with himself, to the married man with a new job and family whose preoccupation with the daily responsibilities of life once again disconnected him from himself, to the palliative care volunteer today who sits with dying patients that open his heart and reconnect him with himself again—a life brought full circle by a trajectory that William Wordsworth captures in his eye-opening poem *"Intimations of Immortality from Recollections of Early Childhood."*

Wordsworth tells us that "our birth is but a sleep and a forgetting," and Soul, our "life's Star," our inner self, comes from "God, who is our home." He calls life a "prison house," and as we grow up we soon forget where we came from. "Shades of the prison house begin to close /Upon the growing Boy," and before long memories of our true home in God "die away /And fade into the light of common day."

Ascended Master St. Padre Pio told me in one of my spiritual healing sessions that I had with my spiritual sensitive for my book *Healing with Padre Pio* that "life is a voyage of discovery," but what do we discover if not our way back to "God, who is our home"?

The trajectory of Gary Davis's life points to this voyage of discovery, although he doesn't quite see it like that. The whole thing puzzles him. He admits that he doesn't have any answers and that he doesn't belong to any spiritual path or has an agenda when sitting with dying patients; it's enough for him to just sit and be in the moment with them. These special moments connect him with something bigger than himself, and even though he doesn't know what this something is, he feels that he is re-connecting with life, and this gives him a sense of meaning and purpose.

Gary draws a parallel with his experience of sitting with terminally ill patients and his experience with the children he cared for when he was young. Both experiences gave him a sense of connecting with life.

When he worked with children, he felt "engaged with life," a feeling that he began to lose when he left the daycare center and took another job. His daycare work was focused on working from the heart, he said; but his new job was working from the mind, and over the years he began to feel like a stranger to himself again. He felt alienated and disconnected from life; and then he got a phone call from his brother that their father had died.

Three weeks later he got another phone call from his brother, telling him that their mother had died; and Gary said he felt a "nudge" at his back pushing him to the front of the line. He was the oldest sibling, and he felt that it was his turn next to die, and he had to face his own mortality.

This frightened him. Then a friend gave him the book *Who Dies? An Investigation of Conscious Living and Conscious Dying*, by Steven Levine, which inspired Gary to look into spending time with terminally ill patients. He contacted a surgeon friend at the Queensway-Carlton Hospital in Ottawa, who connected him with the person in charge of the volunteer department, and Gary was accepted to become a palliative care volunteer and he was allowed to sit with dying patients—which brought him full circle to his early days of caring for children in the daycare center.

When Gary worked with children he said he didn't have to figure life out. It was just there. He experienced the meaning of life in his work. But after four years of working at the daycare center he had an experience with a four-year old boy that changed his life. The little boy was tugging at his pant-leg, crying for attention, and Gary knew that his heart was no longer in his job, so he moved on to another career.

He got married, had children, and became successful as a business consultant, and then his parents died and he had to stare into the face of his own mortality, and to his surprise his life looped back onto itself when he became a palliative care volunteer...

"Old whore life" has a bag full of tricks, and she will use whatever trick it takes to screw us of our joy of living.

One of her favorite tricks is to keep us so busy that we don't have time to think about why we are here, where we came from, who we really are, why we do what we do, and where we are going. **We are so preoccupied with life that we have no time to experience the simple joy of living,** and eventually we become so disconnected with life that we begin to feel that life has no meaning and purpose apart from what we do; and then we cry the existential blues—*"Is this all there is to life?"*

No, this isn't all there is—despite what brilliant writers like TC Boyle have to say ("life is tragic and absurd and none of it has any purpose at all"). **Life is our way back home to God** (a concept that I'm going to explore in another musing, "Life is the Medium and the Message," which was inspired yesterday as I read Saturday's *Globe & Mail's* tribute to the 100th anniversary of Marshall McLuhan, the author of the famous line "the medium is the message"), but one has to know how to ride the currents of life to find their way back home to God—which Gary Davis found when he "chanced" upon the inherent spiritual wisdom of *doing for others*.

Doing for others stores one's treasures in heaven. This is the spiritual secret that Jesus revealed to the world when he said, *"Lay not up for yourselves treasures upon earth, where moth and rust dost corrupt, and where thieves ("old whore life") break through and steal. But lay up for yourselves treasures in heaven, where neither moths nor rust doth corrupt, and where thieves do not break through nor steal. For where your treasure is, there will your heart be also"* (Math. 6: 19-21).

Doing for others speaks to the human heart, where God resides; and the more we do for others the closer we are to God. This is why Gary Davis felt like he didn't have to figure life out when he cared for children, because he was right there, where God is, in his own heart; and when he gave of himself to sit with dying patients he once again found himself right there, where God is; and without realizing that *doing for others* got "old whore life" (his fear of death) off his back, he once again began to feel the joy of life.

"I had this sense that people who were dying were nothing but who they were in that moment, similar to my experience when I worked with children," he said. "I consider it a success to just be in the moment. That's enough. I'm just there, and that's enough for me."

Because being there, in the moment, he was with God; that's why it was enough for him. He didn't need any more than that to be at peace with himself, because the selfless act of *doing for others* stores one's treasures in heaven, our spiritual home where we all came from and where we are destined to return.

Before I bring this musing to closure, let me share an ironic insight into Gary's experience of becoming a palliative care volunteer.

The first patient that Gary sat with was an eighty-two year old woman called Jane. She had terminal cancer. One day Gary went to sit with her and Jane had photos all over her bed. She was a model in her youth, and when Gary studied her photos he exclaimed. *"Jane, you were beautiful!"*

"Yes, I was," Jane said; "and that was my problem."

Gary didn't understand, and Jane explained. "I was so beautiful that people wanted to be with me all the time. People wanted to do for me. I never did for others, and that's my shame," she said, and broke into tears.

Ironic, isn't it, that the first person that Gary, who had "chanced" upon the ancient wisdom of storing his treasures in heaven by *doing for others*, should sit with an eighty-two year-old woman dying of cancer who in her youth was so absorbed in her own beauty that she never learned the spiritual secret of *doing for others*?

10. Life Is the Medium and the Message

I drove to Waverley Landing Sunday morning to see if they had a copy of Saturday's *Globe & Mail* (July 16, 2011), which I was too late to pick up at my usual place at Wyevale's Jug City on Saturday, and I was lucky to find a copy at Waverley Landing; and the first item that caught my eye on the front page was a tribute to Marshall McLuhan's 100th anniversary. When I got home I sat on the front deck and dove into the article, and the more I read the stronger I felt the tap on my shoulder.

This is the second time my Muse has tapped me on the shoulder to write a spiritual musing on McLuhan's famous saying "the medium is the message," but I'm still hesitant to commit myself; not because I don't want to (I love this challenge especially), but because what my Muse wants me to say about the medium being the message may be too much for my reader, and I'm still hesitant to commit myself.

But my Muse was insistent this time, almost making me feel guilty for putting it off, and it's only fitting that I take on this challenge now seeing that Thursday is the 100th anniversary of Marshall McLuhan's birth…

Marshall McLuhan was a communications expert who gave us the term "global village." He has been credited for foreseeing the Internet 30 years before it was invented, broadcasting scores of ideas in his Delphic manner about how electronic communications media was changing the way humans think. He was a professor of English at the

University of Toronto's St. Michael's College for 34 years, and his most popular book is *Understanding Media* (1964). He died in Toronto in 1980.

Michael Valpy writes in the *Globe*: "McLuhan believed that each new technology created a new human environment and thus a new way of thinking. The medium-is-the-message meant the content of electronic media is insignificant; it is the medium itself that has the greater impact on the environment. In other words, it wasn't what we were seeing on TV that was important; it was the fact that we were watching TV (and not doing other things) that altered our brains."

In order to capture the elusive insight that my Muse wanted me to write about in my musing, I needed the right entry point, but none of the titles that I came up with for my musing seemed right; so I gave up and said to my Muse, *"You want me to write this, give me the entry point!"* And, to my surprise, my Muse gave me the entry point I needed while I was in mid-thought writing my last musing—*"Life is the Medium and the Message."*

My whole insight was contained in this title, and now it's my job to creatively work it out for my reader…

Life is the medium and the message is such a power-packed spiritual insight that it's going to chafe "old whore life" like nothing I've written yet—and I chafed her many times in the first edition of my musings, *Just Going With The Flow*; but hey, how many times has she gotten away with screwing us of our virtue?

A word if I may about "old whore life." By now one should know that "old whore life" is my metaphor for the negative forces of life. But, in all honesty, I believe "old whore life" is much more than a metaphor. I believe "old whore life" is a universal archetype that exists in the collective unconscious and can be spontaneously activated the moment it is given an opportunity to address a personal karmic issue—and the older and forgotten our karmic issue is, the more salacious pleasure it gives the "old whore" to settle the karmic score and screw us of our virtue! But why, exactly, do I chafe "old whore life" with my spiritual musings? Why indeed, I can hear one asking?

Well, this is really going to exasperate her, I know; but imagine if you will someone you know well who has a tendency to "put on the dog," as it were; but one day she (or he) goes too far and you say, "Oh for God's sake, stop pretending; you're not fooling anyone but yourself!" And imagine if you will yourself in a social situation when you are *compelled* to tell a lie to save face. And imagine a situation at work when you are given an opportunity to advance your career, but at the expense of your personal ethics. What would you do?

There are endless opportunities for "old whore life" to screw us of our virtue, and we never know when they will arise; but my musings are like a beacon of light cast upon the wily ways of "old whore life," which is why it chafes her whenever I shine the light of consciousness upon her, because I reveal her for who she really is—US!

"Old whore life" does not like to be seen; meaning, we don't like to be found out, and the "old whore" is most effective when she is not seen. Ninety-nine percent of the time she's not seen. This is why she has that smug grin on her face all the time. "How stupid can you be?" she says, shaking her head in laughter for not finding her out.

That's "old whore life," always making fun of us at our expense, and I for one got so tired of being screwed by her that I vowed to do something about it—and I did. I woke up to my own shadow self, and by consequence I woke up to "old whore life"!

How I woke up is a long story, which I've related in my novel **Keeper of the Flame**; and now that I am aware of the games that "old whore life" plays with us I'm obligated as a Keeper of the Flame to shine the light of understanding into those dark corners of the mind where "old whore life" likes to hide from us; and I know that today's spiritual musing is going to blind her like a deer caught in the headlights of an oncoming transport!

Let's begin with **life is the medium.** Medium, in this context, means the means by which to convey, or transmit something. What, then, does life transmit, or convey? According to McLuhan's dictum, life conveys the message.

Actually, for McLuhan, **life IS the message** — because he says that "the medium is the message." So, what message does life convey?

In a word, the Word! This is the message that life conveys: *"In the beginning was the Word, and the Word was with God, and the Word was God. The same was in the beginning with God. All things were made by him; and without him was not any thing made that was made. In him was life; and the life was the light of men. And the light shineth in darkness; and the darkness comprehended it not"* (John 1: 1-5).

So, the big question now is: What is the Word?

It has taken me years of indefatigable effort to penetrate the mystery of the Word, and thanks to my *Royal*

Dictum (a personal ethic of self-denial that I lived by, inspired by Sophocles' play *Oedipus Rex*, Gurdjieff's teaching, and the sayings of Jesus), I parted the veil and caught a glimpse of the Word.

The Word is Divine Spirit, the omniscient guiding force of life. The Word is the creative life force, which creates life and sustains life. The Word is the spiritually reconciling energy of God and the creative energy of God. In short, the Word is the Way, and the Way is life itself.

This is why my Muse gave me the title "Life is the Medium and the Message"—because life is the medium that carries its own message of the Word, which is spiritual self-reconciliation consciousness!

Jesus was living proof of the Word of God, which he reveals when he says, ***"I am the way, the truth, and the life; no man cometh unto the Father but by me"*** (John 14: 6). This was his way of saying that he had awakened to the Word, and through his teachings one could find their way back to "God, who is our home."

What this means, in the broadest and most annoying terms for "old whore life," is that any experience we have in life carries a message of spiritual self-reconciliation consciousness, which means that *through life experiences, the Word teaches us about our divine nature, our true self.*

This is why the Word chafes the "old whore" off, because she does not want us to become aware of our divine nature. "Old whore life" cannot exist in the consciousness of our divine nature. She can only exist in our human self-consciousness, our personality and ego self—and especially in our shadow self, the repressed aspect of our personality where she has all the freedom and power to influence our behavior and screw us of our virtue!

St. John says, *"The life was the light of men."* And he further says that *"the light shineth in darkness; and the darkness comprehended it not."* Looked at closely, St. John is telling us that the light of God exists in the life of man, but man cannot see the light of God in his own life; this is why the "old whore" struts around with that smug grin on her face!

"Old whore life" has been laughing at us since the dawn of man. She can't help herself. This is her nature. But why?

To answer this I have to delve into the metaphysics of spiritual growth—which addresses the very purpose and meaning of life; but I'm not quite sure I should challenge myself with this. I'd rather wait for my Muse to inspire me, because I know that when my Muse wants to get a thought out there, I'm ready to write it.

Having said this, let me sum up today's musing by saying that life itself is both the conveyer of the message and the message, and the message is the Word of God, which is the omniscient guiding force of life that guides us through the snares of "old whore life" whose *raison d'etre* is to keep us trapped in the cycle of karma and reincarnation!

11. A Letter to Padre Pio

Letter to Ascended Master
St. Padre Pio,
Wednesday, July 20, 2011

Dear Padre,

I'm in that in-between state, not quite here nor there, which I've induced by my habit of procrastination, and it occurred to me to write you a letter this morning in lieu of the spiritual musing that I started to write ("No Path Is The Wrong Path") and ask for your help to bridge this peculiar state of consciousness that weighs heavily upon my conscience.

I keep thinking of something that Rebazar Tarzs said in Paul Twitchell's book *The Far Country,* that **we shouldn't substitute one responsibility for another just to avoid doing what we know we have to do,** because this is a subtle form of self-deception; but I'm too aware of myself to let it slip into the recesses of my unconscious, and I feel guilty for procrastinating!

Why do I put off doing what I'm supposed to do by doing something that I feel is more important and love to do—like writing?

I have a long list of things that I have to do for our house that never got done when we built it, and this has begun to weigh heavily upon me. I can no longer justify myself by saying that I was "called" to write another book. That won't cut it anymore.

So Padre, what did you do when you were faced with a similar dilemma, which I'm sure you did because this seems to be a universal human trait? Or is it just me?

I can hear you saying that you took the vow of obedience (along with chastity and poverty), and you did what your superiors told you to do. Your will was not your own, as such, so you never really had to wrestle with this dilemma. You grew into the state of consciousness of doing your superior's will, which was the will of your Holy Mother Church, and ultimately the will of God. But you must have had the dilemma of discerning God's will from the will of your superiors and the Church, did you not?

Yes, I hear you say; and that was your longsuffering test, because I know from reading the dozen or so books on your remarkable life that you were asked to do things that you questioned in your heart, like the time you were ordered to stop writing to your spiritual director, or hear holy confessions which you were so spiritually gifted to hear; but you obeyed. You suffered in silence, and you reaped your "glory" in heaven.

I love your word "glory" for Christ's spiritual principle of storing our treasures in heaven. Your word "glory" spoke to me when we were talking about the spiritual rewards of suffering, because I *knew* what you meant. That's why I enjoyed my spiritual healing sessions with you. You spoke to me, to who I am, and I couldn't get enough of your spiritual wisdom.

Maybe that's why I asked if we could continue our talks for another book next year, because I love being in the company of an Ascended Master. It's such a pleasure to talk with someone who is in that place of all knowing and seeing, because you validate my truth—despite how difficult it was for you to admit to some of the false concepts of your beloved Roman Catholic faith, like eternal damnation in hell!

Of course, one could say that you are a figment of my overactive imagination; an archetypal manifestation like a character in a novel. And I'm sure I will be accused of this when *Healing With Padre Pio* comes out next year. But that's life, isn't it?

If I hadn't worked out the three stages of human evolution—the exoteric, mesoteric, and esoteric stages of spiritual growth that helped me to penetrate the mystery of the levels of human consciousness—I would still be wrestling with Demon Doubt. I would be still seeking truth. I'd still be "groping to be grasped by God," as St. Augustine would say.

This doesn't mean that I found Truth. It simply means that I have wrestled Demon Doubt to the ground with the truth that I have found, and this gives me the confidence to believe that my spiritual healing sessions with you were not with an archetypal manifestation but with you Padre Pio, the humble Capuchin monk from San Giovanni Rotondo, Italy who suffered the holy wounds of Jesus for fifty years and who was canonized by Pope John Paul 11 in 2002.

You lived quite the life, Padre; but you know what? So did I? Because if I hadn't, we wouldn't resonate the way we do. This is why you said that we were very much alike. All roads lead to Rome, as the old saying goes, and our roads, as different as they were, led to the same place—our true self.

But that's the purpose of all roads, isn't it? This is why I proposed another book with you, because I want to introduce the obvious to mainstream literature, and by obvious I mean the concept that all paths lead to God. There are as many ways to God as there are souls. You know this or you wouldn't have given me the image with the three forks in the River of Life, which symbolizes the Way as we live it individually.

But this image of the Way being One River that flows from God through life and back to God is a hard concept to get across to people, because the world has been led to believe that only certain paths will take them back home to God. This is why there are so many religions in the world, and so much contention among the races.

That's okay, though. Everyone is where they belong because that's where their karmic destiny has taken them. In the fullness of time they will see that the Way is one, and their own life the way to their true self, God, truth, salvation, and happiness!

I really don't think I have anything else to say at the moment, so I'm going to sign off. I want to thank you for listening. Of all your virtues, I believe listening to the hearts of others has to be your favorite. After all, it has been said that you listened to as many as five million confessions when you were a humble priest!

Thank you for listening, Padre. Until the next time, I remain your humble companion on this never-ending journey to truth…

Orest,
Bluewater,
Georgian Bay, Ont.

12. Where Does Your Treasure Lie?

"For where your treasure is, there will your heart be also" (Math. 6: 21), said Jesus, which came to mind as I thought of the little sacrifice that I made for Penny yesterday afternoon. It certainly wasn't much, in the grand scheme of things; but I have come to learn over the years that **the whole is reflected in its parts, and the gesture speaks the whole man.** This is worthy of a spiritual musing...

We all have needs, wants, and desires. This is a fact of life. And serving our needs, wants, and desires speaks to the individual; but we don't all have the same needs, wants, and desires. We may share common needs, wants, and desires; but fundamentally we are all different, with individual needs, wants, and desires. This is why we pursue personal goals.

One of my goals has always been writing. As early as grade nine, I wanted to be a writer; but in grade twelve I read Somerset Maugham's novel *The Razor's Edge,* and his hero Larry Darrel sparked a desire in me to become a seeker; and so I began my life-long quest for answers to life's big questions. This became my greatest need, and all of my wants and desires served my greatest need.

But I didn't share this need with anyone. This was a private, secret need, which I couched in my goal of becoming a writer. Writing gave me the freedom to become an eclectic reader, and I explored many different paths, religions, and philosophies in my search for answers to life's big questions, even books on running like *The Psychic Power of Running* by Valerie Andrews. This book inspired me to become a distance runner; but little did anyone know that running served my greatest need.

Doctor George Sheehan, who was called "the guru of running," was one of my favorite writers on running. "In running I found my salvation," he wrote, which puzzled his readers; but it didn't puzzle me because I *knew* what he meant. I, too, had experienced the miracle of "salvation" in running—a secret so mystical that few people can put it to words.

Jesus did, and with aphoristic genius. He understood the secret of "salvation," and he couched it in all of his sayings. When he spoke about storing our treasures in heaven, he was referring to the secret of "salvation" that Doctor George Sheehan discovered for himself through running.

'*Lay not up for yourselves treasures upon earth, where moths and rust doth corrupt, and where thieves break through and steal,*" said Jesus; "*but lay up for yourselves treasures in heaven, where neither moth nor rust doth corrupt, and where thieves do not break through or steal*" (Mat. 6: 19-20). And then he reveals the "secret" of the mystical process of "salvation" (spiritual self-realization consciousness) that is couched in his teaching: "*For where your treasure is, there will your heart be also.*"

Running had become Doctor Sheehan's "treasure in heaven," which could not be tarnished by life nor stolen by anyone because it was beyond the grubby grasp of life.

His "treasure" (the individualized consciousness that he realized from his experience of running) could not be tarnished nor stolen by life, because it existed beyond the reach and grasp of life; it existed in that mystical realm that Jesus called "heaven," and by this he simply meant a higher state of consciousness beyond the realm of physical life.

This is a deep mystery, one that theologians have been wrestling with for centuries; but only mystics understand it. St. Padre Pio was a mystic who suffered the stigmata for fifty years. He understood the secret of "salvation." He knew that "salvation" could be realized through self-sacrifice. That's why he called self-sacrifice his "glory." "Glory" was Padre Pio's word for the "treasure in heaven" that he realized through self-sacrifice.

I understood Padre Pio. I, too, had learned the mystical "secret" of self-sacrifice. That's why I smiled to myself yesterday when I was reminded of Christ's quotation about storing our treasures in heaven when I made the little sacrifice for Penny and took her for coffee instead of going back to my van and listening to Paul Kennedy's program on Marshall McLuhan, who had excited my curiosity enough to write a spiritual musing on his famous saying "the medium is the message."

I had just finished writing for the day and I was going to meet Penny for coffee at Wal-Mart around one-thirty, but on my drive to Wasaga Beach Paul Kennedy's show *Ideas* was on the radio. It was a documentary on Marshall McLuhan , and it was so interesting that I thought of parking the van somewhere and listening to the whole show, but Penny was expecting me and I had to forfeit the program.

"*Ideas* was on the radio as I was driving in," I told her, as she put her work bag under one of the card bins

(Penny's a Hallmark Card rep). "It was on Marshall McLuhan. You know, the medium-is-the-message guy."

"Do you want to listen to it? We can have coffee later," she generously offered.

I smiled. "I used to have priorities, sweetheart; but now I have you."

Penny laughed. That was a code message that meant I would forfeit the show to be with her because she was my first priority, and we went to McDonald's for a coffee. How I came to the realization that Penny was my first priority is a story in itself; so, if I may…

When Penny and I got together twenty-three years ago, I was used to my bachelor ways with three very definite priorities that governed my time and energy: my work (I was a self-employed painting contractor), my love for writing, and distance running.

Without going into detail, I had to give up long distance running after eight years, so Penny had one less priority to compete with in our relationship; but she did come to the realization that writing was very important to me, and although it bothered her that I placed writing above our relationship she finally learned to live with it.

When we moved to Georgian Bay seven years ago I was so busy in my work contracting that I got up every morning around three thirty and wrote till I went to work at nine, and my morning time was precious to me because I'm a morning writer; but one morning Penny came into my writing room and asked if she could have coffee with me.

"Of course," I said, and we had coffee together; but she knew how precious my writing time was and didn't prolong our coffee time.

The next morning we had coffee in my writing room again, and the morning after, and I didn't deny her the joy of our morning coffee time, and this went on for a week or so; but one morning she wanted to stay longer and asked if she could have another cup of coffee with me.

I swear to God, the words just leapt out of my mouth: *"Sweetheart,"* I said, *"I used to have priorities; but now I have you. Of course you can have another cup of coffee with me."* And I went downstairs to refill her cup.

This gesture deeply touched Penny, because she knew how precious my writing time was to me, and it's become a code message for the sacrifice I make for my love for her—like sacrificing the documentary on Marshall McLuhan that had engaged my interest.

I admit that there was a moment of hesitation when she gave me the choice of going back to the van to listen to my show, but as Jesus said, ***"Where your treasure is, there will your heart be also."*** Penny was my treasure, and I wanted my heart to be with her, so I forfeited my desire to listen to my radio show…

Having said this, let me see if I can demystify the hermetically sealed mystery of "salvation" that Jesus couched in his sayings, especially his cryptic saying of storing our treasure in heaven.

Gurdjieff's teaching of "work one oneself" awakened me to the realization that by "treasure in heaven" Jesus meant a special type of consciousness that one realized by living life a certain way. This special type of consciousness is the spiritualized consciousness of our ego self, which I had learned how to transform by "working" on myself with Gurdjieff's techniques of *non-identification, self-*

remembering, voluntary effort, and *conscious suffering.* These techniques taught me the fundamental spiritual principle of Christ's teaching, which was self-sacrifice. ***"He that loveth his life shall lose it; and he that hateth his life in this world shall keep it unto life eternal,"*** said Jesus (John 12: 25), which sums up the process of spiritualizing one's ego consciousness and earns one the right to enter into the "kingdom of heaven."

Padre Pio, who suffered the holy wounds of Jesus for fifty years, came to the realization that self-sacrifice transforms the consciousness of one's ego self and spiritualizes it, which is why he always said that he suffered for the glory of God. This was his way of saying that he stored his treasure in heaven also, and why he called this precious treasure his "glory."

I had my own word for this special type of consciousness that one created by self-sacrifice; I called it "virtue." And the more "virtue" I created, the more I grew in spiritual self-realization consciousness; and the more I grew in spiritual self-realization consciousness, the more spiritual gravitas I had, and this began to affect people in a funny way, and still does.

It's very difficult to convey why people are affected the way they are by people who have spiritual gravitas, because this is a metaphysical reality that cannot be empirically proven; but I've experienced it so often that I know that people who realize more spiritual gravitas than the rest of society will threaten the ego consciousness of society—which is why the great spiritual leaders of the world have always been persecuted.

In other words, it takes a lot of wisdom to live in the world when you have realized a level of spiritual goodness that exceeds society's tolerance level for goodness—which isn't very high these days because we have become so self-absorbed!

If I may then, let me bring this musing to closure with a remarkable little coincidence that happened the day after I forfeited my radio program to have coffee with Penny.

It was sweltering that day, as it had been for the past few days, and Penny came home from work with a new beach umbrella and body board, so we packed a couple of bottles of cold water into our little cooler, my notebook and a magazine that I picked up at random from the pile I had on our stairs, and we drove down to the beach and set up our new umbrella and folding chairs and Penny went in for a cold dip to try out her new body board and I read an article on mindful living in *Utne Reader* magazine, "You're Grounded," by Matt Sutherland, about "connecting with the earth to cure pain."

After her swim we went for a wonderful beach walk and got "grounded" (how coincidental that I should chance upon an article that explored the health benefits of "grounding" yourself, like doing a beach walk which, to my surprise, gave me the best night's sleep I had in a long while!), and then we packed up and headed for home.

As we were walking the long boardwalk up through the sand dunes, I thought about how fortunate I was for making Penny the first priority of my life and how such a simple thing like joining her on the beach made her happy. She was like a little girl in the water, and I even said to her when she came out, "It's nice to see the little girl in you come out to play. We should have done this years ago, sweetheart."

But we were so busy building our new house and starting our life over in Georgian Bay that we really had no time to enjoy the bay, and that was the first time we had brought our chairs and actually enjoyed a couple of hours together on the beach; and as we walked the boardwalk to our car I thought about forfeiting the radio show the day before and taking the time to enjoy our sandy Georgian Bay beach with Penny and the idea struck me to write a spiritual musing on storing our treasure in heaven.

I shared this with Penny, and she said, "You should."

Just then, as "coincidence" would have it, a beautiful woman in her late twenties or early thirties who was coming down the boardwalk talking on her cell phone said, *"Plant the seed and see where it goes—"*

That's all I heard, but it was more than enough because I *knew* that it was the language of life giving me confirmation to go ahead with my musing; so, being a servant of my Muse, I've planted the seed; and where it goes, I really don't know.

13. The Fear of Waking Up to Old Whore Life

I think it's time to do a spiritual musing on "old whore life," that elusive, curious creature whose name is legion…

Have you ever had the experience of someone pointing out something about yourself (something you said or did) that you instinctively denied? Your husband, wife, mother, father, friend, or co-worker said something that did not reflect well on your character?

We deny it because that's not who we are; and we justify and rationalize our behavior with passionate conviction. One day however, when our guard is down, our focus shifts for a fleeting moment and we catch a glimpse of "old whore life" and recoil in disgust.

It's like looking in the mirror and seeing our face in a different light, and it's not as handsome or beautiful as we thought, and fear grips us. "My God," we say, with a gasp, "where did those wrinkles come from?"

As the saying goes, time waits for no man, and we are all affected by the ravages of "old whore life" despite all the cosmetic surgeries and futile efforts to slow down the biological clock. Mortality is a fact of life, and no one can escape death; and if we don't believe in an afterlife, we can embrace our mortality and make the most of life, or we can go to our grave with a bitter rant at the "old whore."

Simon Critchley, a philosopher and author of *How to Stop Living and Start Worrying*, insists that we will live better if we start learning how to die. "The idea that human beings can overcome the human condition has been with us a long time. What enslaves human beings is a longing for immortality. Paradoxically, freedom does not exist in the absence of constraint. To live a free life is to accept the limit of one's human life, which is death. To live in perpetual hope of immortality is to be a slave," he said in the *Psychology Today* interview (June 2011). This is why many people embrace the concept of immortality that religion offers; but what if there is truth to this? What then?

"Old whore life" would like us to believe that this is all there is to life, and she will do everything to keep us asleep to the reality of our immortal spiritual nature; but waking up to the "old whore" is not for the faint-hearted. "Only the most courageous will find their way to God," said Paul Twitchell in his book *The Far Country*.

Gurdjieff, my first mentor in my search for my true self, taught a personal system of transformative thought that changed my life. His teaching forced me to wake up to "old whore life." So difficult was his teaching however that many of his students walked away from it; and some who did try to wake up to the "old whore" ended up taking their own life because the "old whore" broke their spirit.

Gurdjieff believed that we all have a false personality, which revolves around what he called a "chief feature." But our "chief feature" is so well concealed in our personal unconscious that we cannot see it. Ironically, our "chief feature" is visible to the world, and sometimes people will point it out to us. But we don't want to see it, because to see our own falseness is to take responsibility for it, and few people have the courage to do this; hence the fear of waking up to "old whore life."

Ironically, the false we see in others often turns out to be the false that we refuse to see in ourselves. ***"And why beholdest thou the mote in thy brother's eye,"*** said Jesus, ***"but consider not the beam that is in thine own eye?"*** (Math. 7: 3), which was his way of saying that we can see the "old whore" in others but not in ourselves.

Gurdjieff also believed that not everyone is born with an immortal soul, but one could create his own soul if he knew how. This was the premise of his teaching, how to transform our consciousness and create our own immortal soul; but this was next to impossible to do. This is why his teaching broke so many students. It was too extreme.

I took Gurdjieff at his word and lived his teaching as though I had to create my own soul; and I did experience that moment of spiritual consciousness that Jesus called being born again, so I know Gurdjieff's teaching worked. But I had to transform my false self to realize my true self, and in my self-transformation I woke up to "old whore life."

Once I woke up to the "old whore" I saw that Gurdjeiff was wrong to believe that not everyone is born with an immortal soul, because we are all sparks of divine consciousness, and the whole purpose of life is to grow in self-realization consciousness until we become aware of our divine nature, which, ironically, Gurdjieff's teaching helped me do; and it doesn't matter how many lifetimes it takes to wake up to our divine nature, we will all get there eventually. As Paul Twitchell said, "If you don't get it right in this life, you will just keep coming back until you do."

It doesn't matter which life we live however, we still have to break the hold that "old whore life" has on us; and we can never break free until we're willing to accept responsibility for "old whore life"—which is a concept that scares the hell out of us!

It's been years since I lived Gurdjieff's teaching and found my true self, and over time I have grown to appreciate why "old whore life" keeps us asleep to our divine nature; but that's something I can talk about in another musing. For now, suffice to say that we're afraid to wake up to "old whore life" because we're afraid of what we might see.

14. And So It Came to Pass

A long time ago, no one knows quite when, a young man with an adventurous spirit but very innocent to the ways of the world was seduced by Old Whore Life. She became pregnant and gave birth to a male child, whom she named Murphy.

Born of innocence and deception, Murphy was not a normal child. Cursed with his mother's insatiable desire to deceive the world and blessed with his father's guileless nature, Old Whore Life weaned her favorite child for his destined purpose to test the spirit of man with what over time came to be known as "Murphy's Law," and so it came to pass that regardless of what we do in life if anything can go wrong, it will...

For years I puzzled over why some things come easily to some people and difficult to others, because I've always been resentful of those to whom things come easily. I've since grown to not be resentful of the naturally gifted, because I have awakened to how the Spiritual Laws of life work and I now understand that we earn our gifts by how we choose to live our life. But herein lies the problem, because most of us have to fight through all the "bullshit karma" that we have created to realize our own natural gifts!

This has been my problem—fighting through all my "bullshit karma" to get to that state of innocent consciousness where I won't have to keep struggling with "old whore life" and her favorite child's cursed blessing—Murphy's Law!

Thank God I'm stubborn, because had I not this never-say-die attitude "old whore life" would have broken my spirit long ago. But I have broken through the barrier and seen the wisdom of the Divine Plan of God, and I know that even the "old whore" serves a purpose in the evolution of human consciousness, and this purpose is what these spiritual musings are intended to make clear, one inspired musing at a time.

If I may then, let me explain what I mean by "bullshit karma" before I get on with how Murphy's Law frustrated my day yesterday.

My father was cursed with tons of "bullshit karma." Nothing seemed to ever go right for him his whole life, and he would curse his own Calabrese variation of "as flies to wanton boys are we to the gods, they kill us for their sport"—"*managa la miseria!*"

In a word, my father was "jinxed." And he knew that he was "jinxed." That's why he always made the sign of the cross every time he would start a little carpentry project to ward off the "evil spirits" that "jinxed" him.

Born in southern Calabria, Italy into a superstitious Roman Catholic family, my father inherited his family "jinx," which he passed on to his children in the family shadow; hence my befuddlement whenever something went wrong in my life for no apparent reason; but as I became wiser in the ways of the world I learned that this was all Murphy's fault. Little did I realize however that I gave Murphy all the latitude he needed to "jinx" my life; hence the reason our lawn tractor snapped the belt yesterday.

And now I have the inconvenience of asking my neighbor (who is in Toronto at the present and I don't know when he will be back) if he will haul my tractor lawn mower on his trailer again to the mechanic who replaced the belt and did other repairs on it last year, and all because I failed to wash down the lawn tractor with the hose before putting it away into the garage until the next time I had to mow the lawn. All the accumulated cut grass in the undercarriage inhibited the blade and forced the belt to snap, or so I reasoned.

The belt didn't have to snap, but the conditions were there for something to go wrong, and it went wrong—which is what Murphy's Law is all about. Now, this may sound strange and off-the-wall, but I honestly believe the belt would not have snapped had I not been "jinxed" with the kind of "bullshit karma" that called upon Murphy's Law to manifest itself in my life; and that's my spiritual musing for today...

It's all a question of consciousness. "Bullshit karma" is unresolved, disruptive, jinx-making consciousness; and as long as we have enough of this "bullshit karma" to initiate Murphy's Law, we will always suffer the indignity of things going wrong in our life. So, how do we get rid of this "bullshit karma"?

If I may, let me approach this analogously. Given that cigarette smoking has been scientifically proven to cause lung cancer, we can say that cigarette smoking causes "cancer-making karma"—which is what "bullshit karma" is all about, really.

When I got into the habit of making kissing stops at stop signs, I created what I came to call "kissing-stop karma," and when I had created enough of this "bullshit karma" I got pulled over by an OPP officer for failing to make a proper stop, and I had to suffer the indignity of a one hundred and ten dollar fine.

This can apply to anything we do; which means that the kind of karma that we create will attract its consequent effect into our life—i.e., compensatory karma, which balances out the energies of life. So if we create the opposite of "bullshit karma," which can simply be called "harmony karma," our personal consciousness will not be dissonant with the consciousness of life, and things will go much more smoothly in our life; which means that "old whore life" will have to respect us and leave us alone!

Of course, creating "harmony karma" demands the courage to break those habits that create "bullshit karma," the wisdom to recognize the difference between the two kinds of karma, and the time and effort to do the best that we can possibly do in whatever we do so that we don't give Murphy a chance to manifest his *blessed curse*; and it is a *blessed curse,* because through Murphy's Law we become aware of our shortcomings!

In short, we have to change the values that we live by to keep "old whore life" off our back. Indeed, life is all about waking up to how "old whore life" works…

15. A New Species of Man

I enjoy reading Shirley MacLaine. She's a seeker who has explored the road less traveled and shared her spiritual journey with the world. It takes courage to put yourself out there like she has, and she has won my admiration and respect.

I read her latest memoir *I'm Over All That And Other Confessions* several months ago, and something she said immediately inspired a spiritual musing; but I had no time to work on it then, so I made a note in my musings notebook: "When I was in Peru doing *Out on a Limb* (the movie, based on her book by the same title, which I also loved), the Peruvian shamans told me that a new species of Homo sapiens was about to appear. They called the new humans 'homo luminous.' They told me that the forerunners for homo luminous were already among us," wrote Shirley MacLaine (p. 171).

This did not surprise me. In fact, the very name "homo luminous" suggested what I expected the next evolutionary jump would be—a more spiritually enlightened human being. The genetic evolution of man is such a slow process that it will take eons for man to evolve physically into a new species of Homo sapiens (if we don't destroy ourselves first), but spiritually man has all the room in God's kingdom to evolve, and this is what I believe the Peruvian shamans meant with their comment about *homo luminous.*

But what would *homo luminous* look like? Would he look like the rest of us? Jesus looked like the rest of us. He was definitely a spiritually enlightened being. Buddha looked like the rest of us, and he was spiritually enlightened, as was Mohamed, St. Paul, and hosts of other souls who don't have a public profile; so it would follow that there are degrees of spiritual enlightenment depending upon how much one grows in the spiritual life.

The Peruvian shamans said something else to Shirley MacLaine that sparked this spiritual musing: "A new human was emerging, one that would possess qualities that we do not now have. That is because the qualities of space-time have not been advanced before. They said our spiritual existence is a unique combination of free will and predestination. We each came in with a destiny, but free will can pull us out of alignment with that destiny. That is why it is necessary to be in touch with our true self. The true self is totally in touch with the movements of space-time and never fixed in either time or space" (p. 171).

That spoke to me, because I understood exactly what these shamans meant by free will and predestination — because I had worked this out in my novel **Keeper of the Flame.** That was the story of how I aligned my free will with my spiritually predestination; so, if I may, let me do a spiritual musing on *homo luminous*, a new species of man...

To understand what the Peruvian shamans meant by *homo luminous*, we have to put the evolution of man into a context that will allow for the paradoxical coexistence of man's free will and his spiritual predestination, and this context would be the Divine Plan of God.

There is no way to prove this empirically (which is why Gurdjieff said that there is only self-initiation into the mysteries of life), but man is born with a spark of divine consciousness that is pre-destined to evolve and become conscious of its divine nature. Man is also born with free will, so it is man's choice to align his life with his spiritual predestination. But it takes many lifetimes for man to become aware that his spiritual evolution is entirely dependent upon the kind of life that he chooses to live, which is why Gurdjieff said that nature will only evolve man so far and then he must take evolution into his own hands, and if we don't get it right in this life, we will just keep coming back until we do, said Paul Twitchell, re-enforcing the Spiritual Law of Reincarnation.

The Peruvian shamans said that free will could pull us out of alignment with our spiritual destiny, and it is up to us to align ourselves; but given man's preoccupation with satisfying his every desire today, we have pulled ourselves so far out of alignment with our spiritual destiny that we are in danger of destroying planet Earth. This is what the Nine Enlightened Beings revealed in the shocking book *The Only Planet of Choice,* by Phyllis V. Schlemmer; and to correct this they strongly suggested that we learn how to "remove self from self"—which is exactly what the spiritual teachings are all about!

This is why the Spiritual Hierarchy in charge of running the universe has intervened in the evolution of planet Earth with an infusion of spiritual energy that is raising the consciousness of man enough to see that we are responsible for what we are doing to ourselves and our planet, and we can no longer avoid the connection with climate change and our environmentally polluting ways of life; but what exactly does it mean to "remove self from self," because this is the solution to our existential/spiritual dilemma?

To "remove self from self" we have to define our dilemma, which has been the source of much philosophical contention because there is no way to prove that we have two selves—one human and one spiritual. However, the further along one gets on what St. Padre Pio calls this "journey of the self," the more one will see that we do have two selves, which can simply be called our human, or ego self and our spiritual, or soul self. And our dilemma is that our ego does not want to conform to our spiritual self's predestined purpose, which is to become spiritually self-realized, God conscious beings.

Ego loves life, and it wants to indulge in the pleasures of life, which is all part of God's Divine Plan because this is how souls grow in spiritual consciousness. Soul needs the ego energy of life experience to grow in self-consciousness, but when one has grown enough in self-realization consciousness one will begin to feel a pull to the Higher Worlds of God. This is apparent when people say, "Is this all there is to life?"

The sense that there has to be more to life than indulging ourselves in the pleasures of life is soul waking up to its predestined purpose, which is to realize our Divine nature; and herein lies man's dilemma: ego does not want to deny itself the pleasures of life that keep us from realizing our spiritual destiny. Hence man's inherent struggle with himself, and the reason we refuse to align ourselves with our predestined spiritual purpose.

So when the Enlightened Beings tell us to "remove self from self" they are telling us to bring our ego into alignment with our spiritual self, and the only way to do that is to bring some measure of balance, or harmony between them—because it is this overindulgence of our ego self that is the source of our personal, social, and environmental problems.

It follows naturally then, given the logic of spiritual growth through the natural process of life (karma and reincarnation), that the person who consciously aligns his ego with his predestined spiritual purpose will merge the two selves into one self which will shine with the spiritual light of his Divine nature—*ergo, homo luminous!*

The new species of man lives among us, then. He could be anybody, like Victor L. Wooten, author of *The Music Lesson: A Spiritual Search For Growth Through Music,* who was touched by the Holy Flame of God and is now a Keeper of the Flame; or he could be someone like Carolyn Myss who has also been touched by the Holy Flame of God and now seeks to inspire others to "enter the castle of their soul" and become enlightened spiritual beings, or someone like Andrew Harvey whose mission is to awaken people to "sacred activism"; or he could be your next-door neighbor who is so far along on his journey that he has realized his divine nature. He could be anybody who has found their true self and lives their life in the light of God's purpose, which is to serve God by serving life. In short, *homo luminous* is already here, walking among us!

16. Dimensions of Reality

Every discipline has its own dimension of reality, which will remain a mystery until we experience the reality of that discipline; like mathematics, for example. Or physics, microbiology, the medical sciences, architecture, mountain climbing, poetry, music, spiritual healing, forensics—whatever; all disciplines are an entry point into their own dimension of reality, which leads me to wonder how one can dismiss a person's dimension of reality with very little knowledge or experience of that reality.

"I don't believe in psychics," someone says, with very little knowledge or experience of that dimension of reality. Or, "I don't believe in life after death," another says, without having explored the literature and research on life after death.

But what if one does make a study of a discipline and still refuses to believe in that discipline's dimension of reality, as many skeptics do who study the paranormal and still refuse to believe in the dimension of paranormal reality? What then?

I was watching TV last night when it occurred to me—don't ask me what I was watching that inspired the idea for this musing, but out of nowhere the phrase came to me, *"every discipline has its own dimension of reality,"* and I knew I had to explore it.

I understood what it meant, but exploring it would be another matter, and in all honesty, I don't know where to start. This, then, is today's spiritual musing…

Integrity. That's the word that just came to me. Intellectual integrity, emotional integrity, spiritual integrity—personal integrity, in whatever aspect of one's life; and being a creative writer, I can't help but think of artistic integrity.

I remember "waking" up to the artifice of one of my favorite writers after reading one of his short stories. It intrigued and irritated me to read that critics had labeled Somerset Maugham a great craftsman who didn't quite cut it as an artist, because his novel *The Razor's Edge* had a seminal influence upon me in high school; but after I saw through the artifice of one of his short stories I understood what the critics meant.

If my memory serves me, the short story that opened my window of perception on Maugham's brilliant talent for artifice was called "Red." As I read the story, I was seduced by the imagery that Maugham had created with his skillful use of language. He painted such a credible word picture that I was seduced into believing his story—until I came to the end and snapped out of the author's hypnotic spell!

"I can't believe that," I said to myself. "How could he forget such an experience?" I asked. "That's asking too much of me," and I refused to believe that a man could forget such a passionate love as Maugham had described. The story strained my credulity, and for the first time in my life I knew what was meant by the phrase "artistic integrity."

A story has to have integrity to sustain its own dimension of reality. If it does not have artistic integrity, it will collapse on itself just as Maugham's story "Red" did for me; and by artistic integrity, I mean that the author cannot cheat with the creative process—such as creating hypnotic word images just to seduce the reader into believing the story!

This reminds me of a story told by a skeptical journalist who was covering a story in India and happened to catch a street show of a man charming a rope out of a basket, which a young boy climbed and then disappeared into thin air. The charmer played his flute and everyone saw the rope spiraling out of the basket like a snake and going straight up, and up, and up and then the boy climbing the rope; but a fly landed on the back of the journalist's neck and bit him and he slapped his neck, and this slap snapped him out of the hypnotic spell that the charmer had induced with his flute music and the journalist saw the young boy standing on the ground beside the basket grinning at the crowd!

The charmer had seduced his crowd by inducing a hypnotic spell with his flute, and the crowd saw what they were told to see; but it wasn't real. That's how I felt about Maugham's story "Red." Maugham cast a hypnotic spell on me with his incredible skill for creating images with words, but for some reason the strain of the spell on my credulity was too much and I snapped out of it and saw that the story was an illusion!

Which isn't to say that this story wasn't inspired by a real-life event, which I'm sure it was because Maugham did say in his memoir *The Summing Up* that he could talk with a person for an hour and he could write a story; but, as much as it pains me to admit this, I honestly think the critics were right when they said that he had brilliantly mastered the craft of writing but hadn't broken through into the magical dimension of art.

Integrity: that's what defines art. The integrity of its own reality, whether it has been made up or not. Art is its own dimension of reality, and to realize this dimension of reality the creator has to have artistic integrity—which means that he has to obey the inherent rules of the creative process.

What, then, are these rules—which I now see to be the inherent rules of the GAME OF LIFE, because any dimension of reality cannot be sustained without adhering to the rules of its respective discipline—physics, music, and medical healing for example?

Everything we do has its own inherent rules. Building a bridge has its own inherent rules, and unless one has the integrity to obey these rules (whether consciously or unconsciously, it does not matter), that dimension of reality will not be sustained, because that reality will eventually collapse on itself.

This gives credence to the Spiritual Laws of Karma and Reincarnation, which are life's rules of inherent self-correction. When we break the rules of the GAME OF LIFE, karma is forced to correct us. This is why Paul Twitchell said that if you don't get it right in this life, you will just keep coming back until you do.

And getting it right means that we can't cheat life, because every time we cheat life by breaking the rules we incur a debt with life that will have to be corrected. On the other hand, if we have the integrity to play the GAME OF LIFE by the rules we will access the ultimate dimension of reality that all of life strives for.

By sheer coincidence yesterday afternoon I read the special edition of *Atlantic* magazine, *The Atlantic Fiction*

2011, which speaks to the question of artistic integrity. The Chilean American author Ariel Dorfman (*Death of the Maiden*) wrote a short story called "The Last Copy," about a writer who had his novel *The Heart Thief* published by a vanity publisher and wanted to retrieve all of the one thousand copies that had been sent out because the author didn't want the person who inspired his character in the story to read the novel because she would discover that she was the model for this character and would learn how despicable he was for using her the way he did.

He retrieves all the copies but one, and guess who had the last copy? The woman who inspired his second chapter, which was the only chapter that rang true for the eminent book critic Giovanni Belloccio. Ariel Dorfman created a highly believable story that sustained its own fictional dimension of reality; but the irony is that he wrote a story about a writer who could not sustain the dimension of reality of his novel *The Heart Thief.* "Here's what I think," said the critic Belloccio. "The first chapter, shit. The third, fourth, the fifth chapters, every chapter till the end, including the epilogue, shit."

Belloccio (which means "good eye" in Italian) saw through the artifice of Antonio's novel, but he recognized the artistic integrity of the second chapter and encouraged Antonio to build his novel on that reality—which leads to the tiresome question that writers are plagued with: to write about what you know, or to make up what you write?

Bret Anthony Johnston, the director of creative writing at Harvard University, has an essay in *The Atlantic Fiction 2011* called "Don't Write What You Know," and he argues his case quite convincingly that writers should challenge themselves and lean heavily upon their imagination when writing fiction; but I've since come to realize that **the integrity of a story does not depend upon imagination or the facts of life, but upon the inherent rules of the creative process**—which, sadly, cannot be spelled out!

A writer learns what these rules are as he writes, and some never do; but a writer knows when a story works or not, and that's the only way he can be sure that he has not broken the inherent rules of the creative process.

Integrity: that's the key to the ultimate dimension of reality, and unless one learns how to play the GAME OF LIFE by the inherent rules of life, whatever the discipline he will just keep repeating himself until he snaps out of the spell that "old whore life" has cast upon him and he learns to play the GAME OF LIFE by the rules!

17. Passing "It" On

"If you don't get it right in this life, you will just keep coming back until you do," said Paul Twitchell; but what is this mysterious "it" that we have to get right? This is the subject of today's spiritual musing…

I began this second series of spiritual musings because my Muse wanted me to shed some light on "old whore life," that nasty, capricious side of karma that has never been given the respect it properly deserves because it takes enormous courage to get past the hurt and pain of being screwed by "old whore life."

"Life is an old whore that squats obscenely upon my shoulders just waiting to screw me of my virtue," I wrote in my journal many years ago when I was in the throes of my spiritual quest for my true self. I was living Gurdjieff's teaching of "work on oneself," the sayings of Jesus, and my own ethical imperatives that I had gleaned from all the books I read because I had finally come to the realization that to find my true self I had to *become* my true self; and to *become* my true self I had to grow spiritually—hence my pathological drive to harness all the spiritual energy that I could get any way I could.

That's when "old whore life" made her dramatic appearance into my life, because it is her imperative to keep us trapped in the paradigm of life's recurring cycle of karma and reincarnation, and she will do anything to screw us of the virtue that will set us free from our own karmic prison—i. e., our own ego consciousness.

Gurdjieff also called his teaching "the way of the sly man," and by "sly man" he meant that one had to be very clever to harness the energies of life that he needed to "create" his own soul. Gurdjieff taught one how to "create" his own immortal soul (which was a false premise, because we are all sparks of divine consciousness), and the more I "worked" on myself the more I *became* my true self and threatened "old whore life."

This was the most trying period of my life, and I learned so much about "old whore life" that I began to taunt her. *"Come on, you old whore; let's see how you're going to screw me of my virtue today! Come on, I dare you!"* And I waited. But "old whore life" has her own wily ways, and she always comes when we least expect her.

But I created so much virtue "dying" to my life to "find" my life (as Jesus expressed the holy science of spiritual self-realization consciousness) that I caught onto the devious ways of "old whore life," and I wrote in my journal: *"Satan, you are so crafty that I know not which is you and which is me."* And I put myself on high alert and became hyper sensitive to the ways of "old whore life"—which, no doubt, is why my Muse has given me the inspirational directive to shed some light on the "old whore."

Well, yesterday I had an experience that inspired today's musing, because in my little experience—which happened quite by "chance," to the chagrin of "old whore life"—I was given an opportunity to pass "it" on to a complete stranger when I paid for a basket of plump fresh field tomatoes and half of a baker's dozen of freshly picked sweet corn.

"It" is a mystery. "It" is so elusive that few people can hold onto it for any length of time; and if you do manage to hold onto it, you can be sure "old whore life" will pull out all stops to screw you of your virtue until she either breaks your spirit or you break free of the hold she has on you—which is precisely what happened to me.

I broke free of the hold that "old whore life" had on me; that's why I can shed light on this shadow side of life that few people have the sight to see. So, why not come right out and reveal what "it" is and put the "old whore" out of her misery?

"It" is the Way. "It" is the omniscient guiding force of life, which is Divine Spirit, the Voice of God that calls man to his true self. "It" is the creative life force, the River of God that flows through all of life. "It" is the "water of everlasting life" that satisfies man's thirst for God. "It" is the virtue of goodness, honesty, kindness, charity, compassion, and forgiveness. "It" is doing the right thing at the right time. "It" is the key that opens the door to the prison of human consciousness, and the bane of "old whore life"!

"It" is an attitude, a predisposed way of living one's life that chooses the inherently self-transcending spiritual way of life over the self-serving material way of life. "It" is the conscious spiritual life. "It" is an individual path back home to God!

As I said, I passed "it" on yesterday; but the elderly lady that was working at Johnson's Market didn't know that I had passed "it" on to her. Not consciously, anyway. On a soul level, she knew; and that's all that mattered.

And it was humorous. It's always humorous when we catch "old whore life" trying to screw us of our virtue. In my story, the "old whore" tried to seduce me of my virtue of honesty by having me take an extra Italian crusty bun without paying for it; but Divine Spirit alerted me to the "old whore." Here, then, is the little incident that I shared with the elderly cashier at Johnson's Market…

When we lived in Northwestern Ontario, Penny and I did our bi-weekly grocery shopping at the Real Canadian Super Store in Thunder Bay. When we got to the bakery department that Saturday morning, I picked up some fresh crusty Italian buns. They sold by the dozen, but I threw in an extra bun. "A baker's dozen," I said to Penny, and laughed.

In the old days whenever someone bought a dozen buns, the baker would often throw in an extra bun for good will, and this came to be known as the "baker's dozen." However, this wasn't the old days, and throwing in an extra bun and calling it a baker's dozen didn't justify the theft of the extra bun. "Old whore life" would like us to believe that we've done nothing wrong. "What's an extra bun, anyway" she whispers into our ear. "They can afford to give away an extra bun. After all, look at all the groceries you're buying…"

It's very easy to be seduced by the "old whore," and I was that day; that's why it didn't bother me that I had stolen a bun from the store. But then something happened to prick my conscience, and I woke up to "old whore life." The cashier was ringing our groceries through the cash register and everything was going smoothly when suddenly the cash register ceased up. It just stopped!

The girl couldn't figure out what happened. She played with the cash register, but couldn't get it going again. She called another cashier, but they couldn't figure out what was wrong, so they called the head cashier. She came over and tried to figure out why the cash register had ceased up, but to no avail; and then I noticed it—

"It's the baker's dozen. It'll do it to you every time!" I said, and broke into an ironic chuckle; but no one else caught on—except for a man standing third in line. He knew what I was referring to—and just then the cash register started working again!

What are the chances of the cash register ceasing up the moment the cashier punched in the bag of Italian crusty buns? And then unceasing the moment I made the connection? The odds are outrageous. This is why I know that it was Divine Spirit waking me up to the wily ways of "old whore life"!

I had stolen a bun, and I had incurred a karmic debt with "old whore life" for my theft, but Spirit alerted me to my karmic indiscretion, and this made such an impression upon me that I have never done anything like that again; but how I came to share my story with the elderly lady at Johnson's Market was so opportune that I knew Spirit was telling me to pass "it" on—and by "it" I mean the incident that woke me up to the spiritual reality that a theft is still wrong no matter how small the theft may be.

I had dropped by Johnson's Market to see if they had any field tomatoes, because Penny and I were going to a potluck lunch on Saturday. We were having our monthly book discussion class in the morning, and then we were going to have a potluck lunch and I suggested to Penny that if I could find a basket of field tomatoes we could bring Italian Bruschetta with a toasted fresh Italian baguette.

When I pulled into the parking lot at Johnson's Market I saw a table outside full of baskets of field tomatoes, and fresh corn. The tomatoes were selling for $4.99 a basket, which was an excellent price, and the sale sign for the corn read: Baker's Dozen: $5.00.

Thirteen corn were too many for Penny and myself, so I only bought half a dozen; but when I put my basket of field tomatoes and bag of corn on the counter, I said to the elderly lady, "I've got seven corn. Half of a baker's dozen," and then laughed.

She gave me a puzzled look, and I quickly said, "No, there's only six corn. But you don't see that baker's dozen any more, do you?"

"Yeah, the old timers used to sell by the baker's dozen," she replied, and just then I was tapped on the shoulder by my Muse to share my baker's dozen crusty bun story with her, which she rather enjoyed, and it felt really good to pass "it" on to a complete stranger because it was so unexpected...

I thought this was the end of my musing, so I went for my morning shower. I dried myself and lay on the bed to listen to the rest of Q, the CBC morning show. Jian Ghomeshi was interviewing author Ross Perlin on his book **Intern Nation: How to Earn Nothing and Learn Little in the Brave New Economy**, and Perlin said something that I *had* to include in my musing because it gave me a glimpse into the paradoxical nature of "old whore life" that I had not conceptualized yet, and it would bring my musing to perfect closure; *"Internships are a curious mixture of privilege and exploitation."*

Which is precisely what "old whore life" is—a curious mixture of privilege and exploitation: the privilege of being spiritually mentored by life, and the unethical habit

101

of taking from life without paying for it. This requires an explanation.

Perlin's book explores how the marketplace today treats college students that are accepted for internships by corporations. Some students are mentored properly, but many are taken advantage of by companies that exploit them for cheap labor (which speaks to today's ethics in the marketplace); and this whole concept of company-intern relationship sheds light on the paradoxical nature of "old whore life." In short, Perlin's book shows that life is both a giver and a taker.

I said earlier that "old whore life" is a metaphor for that nasty, capricious side of karma that takes without asking, but why is karma nasty and capricious?

Actually, it's not. Karma only appears to be nasty and capricious when we cannot see the connection between the cause and effect of karma, and sometimes we may be so hurt by how life has treated us that we cry foul—like your house burning down, or losing your job.

"Life is so unfair," we lament, pointing our finger at life; but life is karma in action. The two are one and the same. We cannot have karma without life, and regardless what we do in life we create karma that has to be paid back—which sheds light on Paul Twitchell's comment about reincarnation, because if we break the Law of Karma (like exploiting interns for cheap labor) we will have to come back to pay our debt to life, and we will keep coming back until we learn to get "it" right.

So "old whore life" is simply the Spiritual Law of Karma collecting its debts back from us, and as nasty and capricious as she may appear to be sometimes in how she collects these debts (through pain and suffering when we refuse to pay, like your house burning down or losing your job), she's just teaching us the lessons we need to grow in spiritual consciousness until we finally get "it" right—like the lesson she taught me when I took an extra crusty bun without paying for it!

Karma is all about balance. We have to pay for everything we get in life. If we take something without paying for it, life will demand payment someday—be it in this life or the next; so when "old whore life" screws us of our virtue, that's just her tough-love way of teaching us to be honest with life!

18. Old Whore Life: A Literary Device

I've made an observation about creative writing that I have to share in today's musing, because it speaks to the reason why I have called this second edition of my musings *Old Whore Life: Exploring the Shadow Side of Karma*—a title that can be disconcerting for some readers. The truth is that I chose this title purely for literary purposes.

Many writers will write a novel and not select their title until they have completely written their novel, and other writers will have their title before they write their novel. I've experienced both ways of writing a novel, and I learned something about writing that speaks to the mystery of the creative process.

A title speaks to the whole story. It captures the essence of the story, and if a writer has his title before writing his novel his story will conform to his title. Metaphorically speaking, the title is like an empty container that the author has to fill with his story, but the shape of the container will conform the story as the author is writing it. So if the author does not have a title for his story, his story will be free to unfold and give birth to its own title.

This sounds very abstract and metaphysical, but I have experienced writing a novel without a title, writing a novel with a title, and also writing a novel with a title that would not conform to the title and finally it chose its own title. Let me explain.

I wrote a novel called **Soul Talks with St. Paul,** but as I wrote my novel the theme evolved to the point where my story could not conform to its container and finally chose its own title, *St. Paul's Conceit.* My story fit perfectly into this new container, and that's when I realized that *a novel has a mind of its own that gives birth to its own thought.* In this case, my novel gave birth to the thought that St. Paul had a conceit about Jesus Christ that I could not see, but the creative process of the story revealed it to me!

As I explored my insight into the creative process, I soon realized that if I wanted to explore a certain theme—like the concept of the repressed, shadow side of personality—I would have to choose the title of my book first, because the container would then demand of my story to define and conform its theme. This is why I chose *Old Whore Life* for the title of this edition, and for my subtitle I chose *Exploring the Shadow Side of Karma*—because my title would draw out the theme that I wanted to explore (i.e., the unresolved karmic energies of the shadow side of our personality), and my subtitle would give me the latitude that I needed to explore all the potential of my theme.

The central theme of this edition of spiritual musings is the shadow personality; and by this I mean that aspect of our personality that we repress and refuse to integrate into our conscious personality, but which has an enormous influence upon our behavior—like, for example, the Jekyll and Hyde personality. This is an extreme example of the conflicted personality that Robert Louis Stevenson explored in his novel *The Strange Case of Doctor Jekyll and Mr. Hyde*, but it makes the point about the influence that the shadow side of our personality has upon us, despite ourselves.

I wanted to explore the shadow personality, and I knew that if I titled my book *Old Whore Life* the creative process would draw the theme out in my musings. The aspect of the shadow personality that I wanted to explore is the nasty, capricious aspect of our shadow personality that will do anything to keep us trapped in our human consciousness.

"Old whore life" then is a literary device that I have employed to explore the secret life of our shadow personality. In effect, with each spiritual musing I shed a little more light on the dark side of human nature, and I am using the imagery of an "old whore" to illustrate how our shadow personality keeps us trapped in the cycle of karma and reincarnation, thereby inhibiting our spiritual purpose of realizing our true, spiritual nature.

This, of course, presupposes an understanding of our purpose in life, which is to grow and evolve in consciousness until we become spiritually self-realized, God conscious beings; a purpose that can only be proven by the process itself. In other words, as Gurdjieff would say, there is only self-initiation into the mysteries of life, which from my own experience I know to be true; and now I am introducing this self-initiation process into mainstream literature—hence my use of the concept of "old whore life" as a literary device.

The word "whore" means prostitute. It also has a metaphorical meaning. To "whore oneself" is to sell oneself, or compromise one's integrity. *So when I say that "old whore life" will do anything to screw us of our virtue, I simply mean that our shadow personality will do whatever it can to compromise our integrity.* If I may be very crude in what I mean by this, take the vulgar expression "a stiff prick has no conscience."

This simply means that our passions can rule our better judgment, and the more we give in to our passions the more we trap ourselves in our human consciousness. This is why Socrates said that to break free of the prison of human consciousness we have to "gather and collect" soul into herself. And how do we do this?

By living a life of virtue, said Socrates. But this is a very difficult life to live, which is why it takes many lifetimes to break free of the prison of human consciousness. "There is no release of salvation from evil (the shadow) except the attainment of the highest virtue and wisdom," said Socrates in Plato's *Phaedo*. But break free we will, because as the saying goes, ***we will just keep coming back until we get it right***; and the only way to get it right is to break free of "old whore life."

19. Hollywood Goes Esoteric with The Tree of Life

The Tree of Life, the new movie written and directed by Terrence Malick and winner of the *Palme d'Or* at the 2011 Cannes Film Festival, has made quite an impression on critics and audiences alike. I didn't expect to see it until it came out on DVD, but a member of our spiritual discourses class Saturday told us that she had seen *The Tree of Life* last week and was totally captivated by it.

"There was too much to absorb," she said, with a mystified look on her face. "I have to see it again. I've never seen a movie like that in my life."

I had heard Jian Ghomeshi on Q interview Jessica Chastain, who starred as Brad Pitt's wife in *The Tree of Life,* and I recommended the movie to our classmate upon the strength of this interview. Ghomeshi was blown away by the movie, and I had to see it just to see what all the fuss was about; so I kept waiting for it to be released in Barrie, but it never came and I gave up on it. I asked where she had seen it.

"At the Imperial Theatre in Barrie," she said.

"Really? It's in Barrie now?" I asked.

"Yes," she said.

"Where's the Imperial Theatre located?" I asked.

"Downtown. On Dunlop street. I've never been there before. They've got these big reclining leather chairs. It's like watching a movie at home."

"Wonderful," I said, and Penny and I drove to Barrie the following evening. I parked the car just across the street from the Imperial Theatre, and a lady we knew who just come out of the theater waved to us. She had just seen *The Tree of Life* with her elderly friend, and by the look on their face they were still in awe.

I asked what they thought of the movie, but they couldn't put their feelings into words. It was too much for them, and they needed time to process the movie. I told them that I had read all the reviews on the Internet and had my own impressions of the movie, which the elderly lady wanted me to share, so I told her what I felt Malick was trying to do with *The Tree of Life*.

"The basic premise of the movie," I told the lady, in my surmise, "is the story of the evolution of life and the evolution of one specific family; Brad Pitt's family. One of his boys grows up, becomes a successful architect, but then he begins to question the meaning and purpose of life. The narrative appears to be a play between the way of Grace, which Brad Pitt's wife Jessica Chastain symbolizes, and the way of Nature, which Brad Pitt symbolizes; and if that's the case, I can't wait to see the movie because I know from my own spiritual quest that Nature can only evolve man so far, and then man has to take evolution into his own hands—which I believe Malick symbolizes in Brad Pitt's wife, whose love for her family represents the way of Grace which transcends Nature."

The tall, smart looking lady with gray-white hair looked at me with astonishment in her questioning eyes. "You haven't even seen the movie and you told me more about it than I've been able to figure out."

I told her I was a writer and that I wanted to see the movie so I could write a spiritual musing on it for my blog, which piqued her curiosity, so I gave her one of my cards and a brief description of the kind of writing I do. "I think I have an idea where Terrence Malick is coming from," I said, and just then the couple that Penny and I were expecting to join us walked across the street and we all chatted for a few minutes and then the two ladies who had just seen the movie left and the four of us went into the theatre and bought our tickets, and as comfortable as the big soft leather recliners were to sit in, *The Tree of Life* was not a comfortable movie to watch…

We all bring our own "stuff" (intellectual, emotional, and spiritual baggage) to the movies, and sometimes our "stuff" resonates with the movie and sometimes it doesn't. If our "stuff" resonates, we come away from the movie feeling good, affirmed, and even a little smug because the movie validates our life. "Loved it," we say. And if it does not resonate with our "stuff" we come away not caring for the movie. " Hated it," we say.

The Tree of Life is a highly complex, textured movie that has polarized its viewers. Many liked it, and it's my impression that many more hated it. I fall somewhere in between. I liked *The Tree of Life* because it resonated with my "stuff," and I disliked it because I felt Malick was much too heavy on the esoteric dimension of the story, which only the most well-read, spiritually open-minded, and discerning viewers could appreciate.

But then, Terrence Malick is a highly praised filmmaker, and perhaps in his genius he tried to bypass the conscious mind of the viewer and went straight to his unconscious with the powerful (for my liking, a bit over the top) cinematographic imagery of his narrative. But just what is his narrative? Many viewers are still trying to puzzle that out.

I can only speak for myself (from the perspective of my "stuff"), but I see *The Tree of Life* as Malick's valiant effort to lay bare the mystery of life; meaning, through the imagery of his narrative he tried to convey the entire drama of life from the Big Bang Theory of the Universe, to the evolution of Planet Earth, to the evolution of life and man, all the way to the evolution of one particular family of man, and specifically one member of the family who symbolizes man's existential quandary.

"What does it all mean?" we hear Jack (Sean Penn), the oldest son of the O'Brien's (Brad Pitt and Jessica Chastain) for whom a tree was planted to celebrate the birth of their first child, as he wrestles with his conflicted soul—hence the title of the movie, *The Tree of Life* whose roots reach all the way back to the Big Bang where it all started.

This is a big tree. One could call it the Spiritual Tree of Life, which I won't hesitate to do because that's consistent with my "stuff." And this big tree gives birth to all the various trees through the evolution of the universe, all the way up the ladder to the family of man and one particular family tree in 20th Century America called the O'Brien Family.

What makes Malick's movie so captivating is the storyline, which is the story of the O'Brien family woven into the story of the evolution of life, and the underlying theme of both stories is the mystery of life.

This movie shouts, *what does life mean?* The O'Brien's can't figure it out. All they can do is struggle to survive, strive to get ahead, and hope for the best. They are a Christian family that believes in God and goes to church faithfully. Mr. O'Brien even supports his church by tithing his wages, but he can't understand God's plan.

"Life is full of trickery," he tells his son Jack. "You can't be too good if you want to succeed," which is a reflection of how many people who have been beaten down by life feel. They can't trust God. This is O'Brien's legacy to his son. But mercifully Jack has his mother's love and free spirit to balance out his father's cold, authoritative personality.

It's a complicated family dynamic, which in many ways speaks to the family of man; and I'm sure that this was Malick's intent. But then there's another narrative woven into the fabric of these two obvious narratives—the narrative of man's soul.

And this is where *The Tree of Life* loses most of its viewers, because Malick is much too esoteric making his point that there are two ways for soul's evolution in life—the natural, willful way of Nature, and the caring, loving way of Grace, symbolized by Jack's father and mother respectively.

Malick has focused his magnifying glass on one middle class American family in 1950s Texas to enlarge the puzzle of man's purpose in this world, and in Jack, the firstborn son of the O'Brien family who in middle age reflects upon the death of his young brother and the strict way his father treated him growing up—forever striving to teach him how to survive in the world, like all good father's strive to do—is suffering from the angst of spiritual doubt that all people suffer from at one time or another in their life.

Those are the three narratives that I see woven into the plot of *The Tree of Life,* and the first thing I said to Penny and the couple who saw the movie with us was, "That movie is about the spiritual anguish of being trapped in the cycle of life and death. Malick gave himself away in that last scene with all those people walking down into the sea. That's a direct symbolic reference to the Book of Ecclesiastes:—

"'Vanity of vanity, saith the Preacher; all is vanity. What profit hath a man of all his labour which he taketh under the sun? One generation passeth away, and another generation cometh; but the earth abideth forever…All the rivers run into the sea, yet the sea is not full; unto the place from whence the rivers come, thither they return again…'" (Eccl. 1: 2-7).

I didn't quote the entire passage, but I wanted to make the point that I saw all those people walking into the ocean as a visual image of souls returning to the Sea of Life only to be reborn into another body to begin the whole process over again, life after life after life (Malick uses the imagery of a face mask sinking down into the sea to symbolize the old life—the mask, or face of soul's earthly personality—that a soul is dropping and the new life that it would be born into), and the only way to break the cycle of life and death was not by the willful way of Nature, but the loving way of Grace which transcends Nature and takes soul back home to God where it came from before the Big

Bang. And that's the message that I believe Malick wanted to make with *The Tree of Life*.

If I may then, let me explain the way of Nature and the way of Grace, which Malick couched so beautifully in the narrative structure of his movie; but to do this, I have to shed some light on the mystery of soul's purpose in life, which Malick does not offer. Without going into detail then, suffice to say that soul's purpose is to grow and evolve through life experience until it is ready to return home to God.

Thank God there is hope in the way of Grace then, otherwise *The Tree of Life* would be a very depressing movie that simply reflects soul's anguish of being trapped in the recurring cycle of life and death; but there is salvation in Grace, and this is Malick's valiant effort to make sense of the human condition.

If my impression of *The Tree of Life* is correct, that soul is trapped in the recurring cycle of life and death, and the way to break the cycle is to live by the way of Grace, the question is: why cannot the way of Nature liberate soul from the cycle of life and death?

Jesus Christ, who came into the world to give man a teaching of salvation that breaks the cycle of life and death, said: ***"He that loveth his life shall lose it; and he that hateth his life in this world shall keep it unto life eternal"*** (John 12: 25).

Jesus spoke the secret teaching of spiritual liberation in code. In the Gnostic Gospel of Thomas, Jesus said: ***"Whoever finds the interpretation of these sayings will not taste death."*** So, did Terrence Malick break the code of spiritual liberation?

Yes and no. The way of Grace breaks the code, but that's all Malick has to offer. He cannot tell us anything more. Maybe he couldn't tell us anymore. Maybe this is where his own spiritual journey has taken him—right to the edge of life where he looks out over the abyss of the human condition and sees that the only way to cross the hollow of human despair is with love. "Unless you love, your life will flash by," says Mrs. O'Brien.

If love is the key to spiritual liberation (all spiritual teachings believe this to be so), then it might explain why the way of Nature cannot liberate soul from the eternal cycle of life and death—because it's not about love; it's all about survival, which Malick symbolizes in Mr. O'Brien, one of Nature's most evolved species whose whole philosophy is built upon effort of will. "You are the master of your own fate," he tells his son Jack.

He believes that if you want to succeed, you have to take charge of your own life; but ironically his life did not go the way he wanted it to go (he wanted to pursue a career in music), and he's a very disappointed man who does not want the same fate for his firstborn son, the pride and joy of his life. That's why he's so hard on his son Jack; so hard, in fact, that Jack fantasizes about killing his father (Malick even has symbolic references to the Oedipal complex). But his father only wants to make him strong for the enormous struggle of life that awaits him, which redeems his otherwise brutal nature.

But his brutal nature is Nature's primal survival instinct, because to survive in life one has to be strong and fit and ready for all threats to one's life and livelihood. Mr. O'Brien is the head of the household, the leader of his clan as it were, and it is his primal responsibility to see to it that his family survives. Malick couldn't have done a finer job of portraying a father's basic instinct to protect and prepare his family for life, and I'm sure that many viewers will see some primal aspect of their own father in Jack's father.

The way of Nature then is the way of survival. It does not teach man how to love. It can only teach man how to survive. This is why esoteric spirituality maintains that Nature can only evolve man so far and no further. To evolve further, say the spiritual traditions of the world, man must take the way of love—which Malick symbolizes in Mrs. O'Brien—because love transcends the way of Nature and nurtures man's soul until it is strong enough to break the recurring cycle of life and death. As the esoteric tradition says, "When the student is ready, the Master appears."

Jesus appeared, because the world was ready for the esoteric tradition of spiritual liberation from the eternal cycle of life and death; but Jesus couched his teaching in code, which is why he said to his disciples when they asked him why he spoke to the public in parables: ***"Because it is given unto you to know the mysteries of the kingdom of heaven, but to them it is not given. For whosoever hath, to him shall be given, and he shall have more abundance; but whosoever hath not, from him shall be taken away even that he hath"*** (Math. 13: 11-12). This was Christ's way of saying that Nature had evolved them as far possible, and now they had to take evolution into their own hands by living the secret teaching of spiritual liberation, the essence of which is love.

Mrs. O'Brien of course symbolizes the way of Nature also, but she is the nurturing mother who must be submissive to her husband's will, and which Malick portrayed with such stark imagery that the viewer feels sorry for her and comes to her defense; but she can only nurture her children so much with love, because it threatens her husband's natural instinct to teach his children to be strong for life. "You're turning my children against me," he tells his wife after an incident at the dinner table when she came to her son's defense.

Malick was brilliant in his portrayal of the way of Nature and the way of Grace in the role of the O'Brien parents, but both can only do so much for their children; and then, if the children have evolved enough through their own efforts in life, they will be "called" to the secret teaching of spiritual liberation from the eternal cycle of life and death.

"For many are called, but few are chosen," said Jesus (Math. 22: 14), which speaks to the nature of individual choice—the governing principle of man's life. In short, we can choose the natural way of the world—"it's a dog-eat-dog world out there"—and fight and claw our way to the top; or we can choose the way of love—"unless you love, your life will flash by"—and grow in spirit until we are discerning enough to recognize the esoteric tradition that will teach us how to break the cycle of life and death.

The esoteric tradition of spiritual liberation has always been with us, and it has always appeared openly in one disguised manner or another. Socrates openly revealed the esoteric tradition of spiritual liberation in his philosophy. "And what is purification but the separation of the soul from the body, as I was saying before, the habit of the soul gathering and collecting herself into herself, out of all the courses of the body; and dwelling in her own place alone, as in another life; so also in this, as far as she can; the release of the soul from the chains of the body?" he says in Plato's *Phaedo*.

Socrates taught the Way of Virtue, of which Goodness was the highest; and by living a life of virtue soul would break the eternal cycle of life and death. This is the esoteric tradition that Malick points to with the Way of Grace that Mrs. O'Brien symbolizes; but it has to be taken much, much further—and this is always an individual responsibility.

So Malick gives us a choice with *The Tree of Life*: we can choose the brutal way of Nature, symbolized by Mr. O'Brien, and remain trapped in the eternal cycle of life and death; or we can choose the gentle way of love, symbolized by Mrs. O'Brien, and realize our own spiritual salvation. This is their son Jack's quandary. And ours!

20. A Bad Case of Life Fatigue

About fifteen years ago I coined the phrase "life fatigue," because life had worn me down so much that I felt ready to leave this world; but I had a lot more wear and tear in me yet before the "old whore" was through with me. This calls for a spiritual musing.

When I coined the phrase "life fatigue" I had just gone through an incredibly trying experience with a contract I had to hang drywall, tape, and paint seven new houses on the native reserve just outside my hometown of Nipigon. I had been into long distance running for seven and a half years when I got this contract, but this job went sour and burned me out physically, emotionally, and mentally and I was never able to get back into running again—not to mention what it did for my bank account and sleep pattern.

This job caused me so much stress that I became an insomniac, and I haven't had a good night's sleep since. In fact, the best night's sleep I had since that contract was the night of my open-heart surgery three years ago. The first thing I said to Penny when I came too from surgery was, "That was the best sleep I had in my life."

A few years after my contract on the reserve I published my two novel memoirs, and Penny and I suffered so much stress from the negative reaction from our community that we relocated to Georgian Bay, which I will write about some day. I'm still too close to the experience to write about it, but I do have a title that is crying to tell our story: "We May Be Tiny, But We're Not Small." This is a play upon Tiny Township, where we live here in Bluewater, Georgian Bay, and the small-minded people of my hometown.

So the "old whore" got a few more pounds of flesh off me with the publication of my novels *What Would I Say Today If I Were To Die Tomorrow?* and *On The Wings Of Habitat.* And when we moved to Georgian Bay we had a whole new bag of tricks to deal with, and "old whore life" got another chance to beat me down with so much stress from building our new house and starting my business over in an area where I had no contacts and Penny sending out two hundred resumes for a bookkeeping position or related work and ending up with a minimum wage job in a deli where employee morale was so depressing that new employees quit within weeks, which Penny eventually had to do after suffering it out for two years, all leading up to my bypass surgery that knocked me out of commission for two years, and even now I can only do small jobs when I get them; so I'm suffering from a very bad case of life fatigue.

I don't mention all of this to cry foul. (Actually this is only the tip of the iceberg.) "Old whore life" will stick it to us every chance she gets, but I'm so damn conscious of how karma works that I can't cry foul; and, believe me, this really hurts. If I didn't know that I am responsible for my own misfortune, I wouldn't be so damn angry; I'd be angry, but not at myself. I'd be raging at the whole damn world! This is what makes my life fatigue so damn hard to take this time around.

It all came to a head on Friday when I went to the dentist. I went hoping my tooth wasn't cracked from the cherry pit that I accidentally bit into at the spiritual discourse class in Orillia last week, but it was cracked so deep the doctor couldn't save my tooth. I said to him, "If you can salvage my tooth, I'll dedicate my next book to you."

He appreciated the gesture, but he wasn't a miracle worker. St. Padre Pio was the miracle worker, whom I asked to be with me for my appointment; but the only miracle I experienced was the loss of another pound of vanity because the tooth I lost did not enhance my smile one iota. And now I have to get a plate to salvage whatever dignity the "old whore" has left me. I certainly can't afford an implant at four grand or a bridge at three grand; and that's another indignity that I have to own up to for all the precious time that I poured into my writing all of these years instead of my business!

If one of my novels had connected with the public by now I wouldn't mind suffering all of these indignities (our lawn tractor, which only has thirty hours on it and which we unexpectedly poured six hundred dollars into last summer, ceased the blades last week and is in for repairs again—the bearings ceased up, which "smoked" the belt; and I also had to bring my van in for repairs for a new muffler last week), but when I went into the dentist's office Friday expecting a root canal as the worst scenario and came out with one less top front left tooth, I lost it. *"You old whore!"* I screamed in my mind. *"You just can't get enough of me, can you?"*

And it's true. "Old whore life" drools at the mouth whenever she screws a good man of his virtue. Nothing gives her more pleasure. It's that same kind of pleasure that Paul Newman talked about when he told Tom Cruise in one of his hustler movies, "Money won is sweeter than money earned." That's how the "old whore" feels when she screws us of our virtue when we don't expect it—*because we just can't see how we invited it!*

Why did I bite into that cherry pit that led to the loss of my tooth and another pound of vanity? Did I have to suffer such indignity to learn the karmic lesson I was meant to learn? *I curse that cherry pit like Jesus cursed the fig tree!*

This is the theme of my next book with Padre Pio—man's journey through vanity to humility; because this is what life is all about—one big journey through the never-ending dusty catacombs of our own vanity to the humility that finally comes after the totally depressing life fatigue that makes one point his fist to the heavens and curse God!

I saw a painting of a man doing just that. This man had lost his faith and turned on God and did a painting of a man shaking his fist at the heavens. But I could never do that. I've been down that road before in my lifetime as the "scoundrel of Paris" in the mid 17th Century, and I could never do that again; so, what am I to do?

Grin and bear it...

21. The Foul Winds of Life

"Shit happens," people say, which is a vulgar way of saying that sometimes our life can be interrupted by unexpected and unpleasant events.

We've all had these kinds of experiences. They're small annoyances that come with daily life ("old whore life" is just teasing us), and we learn to live with them; but sometimes life throws something at us that knocks the wind out of us, and it may take years before we get it back—if we ever do. Like the accidental drowning of one's child, the random murder of one's parents, or the loss of one's life's possessions by a hurricane that destroys one's house and all of one's belongings but not the house across the street.

This can happen to anyone, and it happens all the time. We don't want to think that it will ever happen to us (the thought alone scares the hell out of us), but when it does happen it feels like a foul wind has blown into our life whose sole intent was to destroy our spirit by taking away what we love most, and we feel betrayed by God.

When a foul wind blows into our life we feel like we've been raped to the core of our being by "old whore life," and there's not a damn thing we can do about it; and then we find out what kind of mettle we're made of. This is today's spiritual musing…

It boggles the mind when bad things happen to good people. It makes no sense whatsoever in our moral universe and it will gnaw at us for the rest of our life unless we find out why the God we prayed to our whole life could be so cruel.

Two men driving down a country road in a stolen car randomly select a farmhouse and break in and murder the elderly Christian farmer and his wife. Why did these men choose this house? How can we make sense of this random act of violence?

Truman Capote wrote a true-life novel called *In Cold Blood*. He explored the murder of a devout Methodist farmer and his wife and two children by two ex-convicts on parole who had heard from an inmate that this farmer had a safe and a lot of money hidden somewhere in his house, which proved to be false.

Capote unraveled the mystery of this senseless crime, tracing it back to the plot hatched by the ex-convicts to break into the farmer's house and steal his money; but their plan went awry when they found no money and they killed the farmer and his family. But how many senseless crimes happen every day that we can't make sense of?

Just because we can't connect the dots does it mean that we are playthings for the gods? "As flies to wanton boys are we to the gods, they kill us for their sport," said Shakespeare. Is there no moral order to our universe?

"There was a man in the land of Uz, whose name was Job; and that man was perfect and upright, and one that feared God, and eschewed evil" (Job, 1: 1), and Satan challenged God to let him tempt Job to test his faith.

God gave Satan permission to tempt Job, but not to take his life; and a foul wind blew into Job's life and he lost all his material possessions, which were great. But Job did not waver in his faith. *"And behold, there came a great wind from the wilderness and smote the four corners of the house, and it fell upon the young* (Job's children), *and they are dead; and I only am escaped alone to tell thee"* (Job 1: 19), but Job still did not waver in his faith.

And Satan blew another foul wind into Job's life and he was smitten with sore boils, but Job's love for God did not waver. But why did God give Satan permission to smite this good man? What did he do to deserve such tragedy?

That's the mystery of life, isn't it?

As tragedies go, Sophocles certainly wouldn't call my experience a tragedy; but why did I bite into that cherry pit that cracked my tooth which had to be extracted? I'd love to explore this to delve into the mystery of the foul winds of life.

Here's what happened. After our spiritual discourse class last month our hostess put out some treats for after-class fellowship. Penny and I brought a cinnamon coffee cake that we had just picked up at the bakery, another member brought a small plastic bag with a piece of Cheddar cheese and some loose crackers, and our hostess put out a small bowl of cherries; the other member didn't contribute anything, as usual; and the hostess had tea, but no coffee. Two members of our class were missing, one lady who seldom brings anything for fellowship and a single parent who is always generous in her offerings.

I placed three cherries onto my plate and a piece of cinnamon cake. I ate the three cherries, placing the pits on the plate, and I took a bite of cake and bit into a cherry pit that was stuck on the bottom of my piece of cake; that's how I cracked my tooth, which I did not suspect was cracked until I went to the dentist because of the pain.

125

It was all very innocent and unexpected, but I could not help but wonder why the cherry pit stuck to the piece of cake and why did it not fall off when I picked it up. It was my first bite, but why did I bite into the pit instead of around it? Was this series of events random chance, or was this experience *"karmically designed"* to teach me something about myself that I refused to acknowledge? Did I give "old whore life" permission to "screw" me of a perfectly good tooth to humiliate and teach me a lesson that I refused to learn?

I believe in karma implicitly. What we sow, we reap. If we sow good, we reap good; and if we sow evil, we reap evil. I also believe in reincarnation. We are all sparks of God that come into the world to evolve and grow in our divine nature.

As we evolve from one life form to a higher life form we are governed by the collective karma of life until we give birth to our own self-consciousness, which I experienced in one of my past-life regressions. The moment we give birth to our reflective self-consciousness we create individual karma that determines the fate of our future lives—which I've written about in my novel *Keeper of the Flame.*

In my novel I connected the dots of some of my past lives to show how our past lives affect our future lives, and how in my current lifetime I came to see that I'm responsible for my own destiny because I am the author of my own karma; and so I sought a way to break the cycle of karma and reincarnation, which I also revealed in *Keeper of the Flame.*

It is impossible to understand why Satan would tempt Job with the loss of his great possessions and children and then also afflict him with sore boils. We're told in the *Book of Job* that Satan told God that Job was only good and upright because he had not really been put to the tests of life, and God gave Satan permission to test Job's faith; but unless we have a better understanding of what Satan is and why he would want Job tested we will never make sense of the foul winds that blew into Job's life.

Satan is an impenetrable mystery. Satan is said to be a fallen angel. In his epic poem *Paradise Lost* John Milton has the fallen angel say, "Better to reign in hell than serve in heaven." Satan is a proud angel. He does not want to serve God. But God is God, the Creator of all; and Satan has no choice but to serve God, which is why he had to ask God permission to tempt Job. But this begs the question: how does Satan serve God?

This mystery took me into the very heart of the secret teachings of the Way. To solve this mystery I had to step out of the paradigm of my Christian belief in evil that kept me blind to how the spiritual laws of karma and reincarnation work; and once I began to discern how these laws work I began to see that we are the authors of our own evil.

And to further shock my Christian psyche, I came to realize that Satan is the "god" (*deus deceptor*) of karma and reincarnation—the divinely mandated ruler of these spiritual laws that keep souls bound to the cycle of life and death, which is what the Gnostics believed. But this begs the question: why must souls be bound to the eternal cycle of life and death? In other words, what is the purpose of reincarnation?

To solve this mystery I had to be initiated deeper into the mysteries of the Way, the omniscient guiding force of life that guides souls back home to God where we came from as un-self-realized atoms of God. My mentor Gurdjieff believed that Nature only evolved man so far and no further. To continue we have to step out of the paradigm of natural evolution and take evolution into our own hands, and we can do this by living the inherently self-transcending values of the Way, which Gurdjieff's teaching of "work on oneself" introduced me to; and as I lived the Way I initiated myself deeper into the mysteries of the Way. This is how I learned that there is only self-initiation into the mysteries of life.

From this gnostic perspective I see Satan as the ruler of the material worlds (the Physical, Astral, Causal, and Mental Planes) whose mandate from God is to keep us trapped in the cycle of life and death until we are ready to take evolution into our own hands, and Satan keeps us trapped by tempting us to create karma that keeps us trapped.

Taking evolution into our own hands means that we have to live the spiritual life, which means that we have to learn how to stop creating karma that keeps us bound to reincarnation. In short, we have to live a life that is inherently self-transcending, which is the conscious spiritual life of the Way.

The conscious spiritual life of the Way understands that Satan is the ruler of these lower worlds whose mandate is to keep souls bound to the cycle of life and death, and to break free of Satan's hold we have to take evolution into our own hands. This is why Satan tested Job. It was Job's time to break free of Satan's hold, which means that Job was ready to break free of the karma that kept him bound to the cycle of life and death.

Job's faith in God did not waver when Satan tested him. In his great suffering, Job burned off the karma that kept him bound to life, because suffering is the slow burning love of God that purifies soul and makes one ready for the higher worlds of God. So the foul winds that blew into Job's life were not evil, as such; they were the winds of his own karma that had to be burned off by the slow burning love of God.

Job's suffering purified his soul. Had Job cursed God for his suffering, he would have lost a great opportunity to purify his soul and initiate himself deeper into the mysteries of life, which is the Way; but because he did not curse God he realized the saving grace of his suffering and was rewarded by God with a new family and greater possessions.

Having said this, I can now ask the question: why did I bite into the cherry pit that caused me so much anguish? Or, to express this in the symbolism of the *Book of Job*, why did Satan have me bite into the cherry pit that caused me personal anguish?

Satan is the lord of karma and reincarnation, so it was my own karma that caused me to bite into the cherry pit that caused me to lose my tooth; but what was this karma? In other words, what did I do to *karmically deserve* the evil loss of my good tooth?

I know the answer to this question, but it will cost me to reveal it because it does not reflect me in the kind of light that I would like to be seen…

To appreciate why I bit into the cherry pit we have to understand that once we make the commitment to live the conscious spiritual life of the Way we automatically put ourselves under the auspices of the omniscient guiding force of Divine Spirit whose purpose is to purify soul and make us ready for the higher worlds of God, which means that our morals and ethics become increasingly more and more refined by Spirit until we are able to discern the subtlest nuances of good and evil—or, the way of Satan and the way of God, to put it in the symbolic language of the *Book of Job*. *"Behold, the fear of the Lord, that is wisdom; and to depart from evil is understanding"* (Job 28: 28).

As excruciating as it may be to admit, I have a character flaw that has been the bane of my spiritual life—I'm a faultfinder. I have traced this character flaw to my past lifetime in London, England. I was an Earl, who abhorred the hypocrisy of the aristocracy, and I mastered the art of singling out the faults of others and slaying them with my rapier wit; and I brought this trait with me into my current lifetime, which has cursed me.

One fault that I thoroughly despise in people is cheapness. And the cheaper a person is, the more I loathe them. I don't loathe them with conscious intent. My contempt for cheapness possesses me, and I have little control over it. In fact, it takes great conscious effort to control my contempt for cheapness.

I could never fathom why I had such contempt for cheapness until just recently when I read the chapter "What Does Love Look Like" in the book *In the Spirit of Happiness*, by the Monks of New Skete. When I read what love looks like, I understood instantly why I have such deep-seated contempt for the petty spirit of cheapness.

"Love looks like generosity. It spends itself willingly (and wisely) for others, be it with time, attention, money, or simply concern," said the Monks of New Skete, and I have

a dangerous facility to spot this lack of generosity in a person, which automatically makes me want to despise them. And the more possessed a person is by this petty spirit of cheapness, the more contempt I have for them; and I have to fight to see their good qualities because this foul spirit of cheapness colors their virtues for me. But why should a person's cheapness bother me so much? What is it about parsimony that I abhor?

Once again, the Monks of New Skete opened up my window of perception. *"What does love look like?"* they ask. And their answer gave me an insight into why I loathe the petty spirit of cheapness. *"Actual love is the willingness to give to others what we would like for ourselves—the golden rule—continually going out from our own limited selves toward the other, unhampered by whatever we might happen to be feeling at the moment."*

In short, I see parsimony as the bane of the spiritual life!

It is customary in our spiritual community to bring a little treat of our choice, baking, fresh fruit, vegetables and dip, or whatever we would like to share during fellowship after one of our spiritual functions, and over the years I've noticed who is generous and who is not; and despite myself I develop an instant dislike for the less generous members. One Higher Initiate whose book discussion class Penny and I attended every month for a whole year never so much as offered us a cup of coffee or tea in any one of our classes!

I could not fathom why I didn't resonate with these members, but I've since come to realize that it's because they don't embody the fundamental principle of the spiritual life—which is unconditional love, or the spirit of generosity

131

that is the premise of our spiritual path. That's why I don't resonate with them, because I can see their hypocrisy; and I have an inherent contempt for hypocrisy that colors my perception of people who make themselves out to be the opposite of what they are, especially members of our community who talk incessantly about being love but whose shadow personality betrays them.

But because I have never been able to overcome my contempt for hypocrisy, Satan ("old whore life") blew a foul wind into my life and I bit into a cherry pit that caused me enough anguish to make me painfully conscious of my habit of spotting this annoying spirit of cheapness in people—which I always do whenever I attend one of our spiritual functions, like the class I attended when I bit into the cherry pit. The annoying petty spirit jumped out at me like a jack-in-the-box when our hostess, who never stops talking about being divine love, brought out a little bowl of ten or twelve cherries with the coffee cake and the few pieces of cheese and crackers, but because I could not contain my contempt for the spirit of parsimony the "old whore" blew a foul wind into my life!

Biting into the cherry pit that cracked my tooth caused me so much emotional anguish that I cannot help but be acutely conscious now of my contempt for parsimony, because my character flaw of fault finding inhibits my spiritual growth; and unless I drop this evil habit and appreciate that "life is a journey of the self," as St. Padre Pio informed me in one of my spiritual healing sessions (which means that I have to stop judging people), I will continue to invite these foul karmic winds into my life.

I'm ashamed to admit it, but I've suspected for a long time that I had to do something about my habit of talking about the faults of others, especially cheapness, because I cannot tell you how many times I literally bit my tongue whenever I vented my feelings for my parsimonious friends and acquaintances; but I never learned my lesson about judging people until a foul wind blew into my life and caused me the loss of a perfectly good tooth.

We can blame Satan or "old whore life" all we want for the tests we suffer in life, but when all is said and done we are the authors of our own misery; and until we realize this we can expect the foul winds of life to continue blowing our way—and more often than not when we least expect them!

22. Love Is Better than Anger

"My friends, love is better than anger. Hope is better than fear. Optimism is better than despair. So let us be loving, hopeful and optimistic.
And we'll change the world."

Jack Layton

I wasn't over my anger yet at "old whore life" when I watched the best three hours of television in my life yesterday—the state funeral for Jack Layton, leader of the Official Opposition to the government of Canada who died of cancer at the age of 61.

In the last federal election (2011), Jack Layton brought the NDP (New Democratic) party from fourth place status (behind the Bloc Quebecois, Liberal, and Conservative parties) to second place, replacing the Liberals as the Official Opposition to the governing Conservatives, and for this he will always be remembered; especially for decimating the Bloc, the separatist party whose only intent in parliament was to break up our beautiful country.

This has to be one of the greatest ironies of Canadian democracy—the province of Quebec elected a group of Bloc MPs whose *raison d'etre* was to separate the province from the rest of Canada and form its own country; but Jack broke the back of this beast in the last federal election, and he will be honored for this monumental service to his country.

Jack wrote a letter to his fellow Canadians just before translating to the other side, a letter that Stephen Lewis, a close friend and colleague who delivered a passionate, elegiac eulogy, called "a manifesto for social democracy." Jack ended his letter with the words "love is better than anger. Hope is better than fear. Optimism is better than despair. So let us be loving, hopeful and optimistic. And we'll change the world."

These words speak to the life of the man, and they touched me so deeply that they healed the anger wrought by that nasty little tempest in my life that started last month with the cherry pit that I bit into that cracked my tooth; and, if I may take the liberty, I'd like to do a spiritual musing on these inspiring words...

What are we here for? Why are we in this world? Reverend Brent Hawkes, who officiated Jack Layton's funeral, said that we are not physical beings who have a soul, but spiritual beings who have a physical body, which is the essential truth of the secret teachings of the Way; but the question remains: what are we here for?

Jack Layton knew intuitively that our purpose in life is to serve our fellow man, because service to life is man's highest calling. "He wanted, in the simplest and most visceral terms, a more generous Canada," said Stephen Lewis in his eulogy.

As I've come to learn in my own quest for the meaning and purpose of life, every person in this world will one day be called to serve life. Doctor Elisabeth Kubler-Ross said in her memoir *The Wheel of Life*: "All destiny leads down the same path—growth, love and service." Jack Layton was called, and he served life in a way that dignifies our fellow man; and the Prime Minister of Canada granted him a state funeral to honor Jack Layton for his enormous contribution to Canadian politics and our democratic way of life.

"He was a lovely, lovely man," said Stephen Lewis. "There was no guile. The public man and the private man were synonymous." And Jack himself told his friend Brent, the Methodist minister who officiated Jack's funeral and celebration of his life, "How I live every day is my act of worship"—which he did by serving his fellow Canadians.

Serving one's fellow man makes one whole; that's the secret of the secret teachings of the Way that Jesus died for. But why are we split? Why aren't we born whole? This is the mystery of the human condition, and which few people ever resolve.

We are not born whole because we are all spiritual seeds of divine wholeness, like the acorn seed is the seed of the oak tree; and it takes many lifetimes of evolution to realize our spiritual wholeness. But to realize our spiritual wholeness, we have to precipitate the process. On its own, Nature will not make us whole. Nature can only do so much for us.

As Reverend Brent Hawkes said, we are not physical bodies that have a soul; we are spiritual beings that have a physical body, and it is our purpose in life to realize our spiritual wholeness; but it takes many lifetimes to realize our true, spiritual self.

Terrence Malick's enigmatically touching movie *The Tree of Life* addressed the question of man's evolution through life. His story spoke of the way of Nature and the way of Grace, the two paths to wholeness symbolized by Brad Pitt and Jessica Chastain (Mr. and Mrs. O'Brien).

Malick realized that the way of Nature can only take man so far on the path to wholeness, because the way of Nature is the way of power, and power cannot nurture man to spiritual wholeness; only love can, the love that is realized by the way of Grace.

Jack Layton knew this intuitively. This is why he wrote that "love is better than anger." Love makes us whole, but "old whore life" will do everything she can to keep us from becoming whole, because "old whore life" does not want us to break the cycle of life and death. "Old whore life" is the way of Nature. "Old whore life" is the way of power, and her purpose in life is to purge our soul of karmic impurities in the hot fires of the trials and tribulations of everyday life. This is why "old whore life" can be so cruel and unfair.

In his eulogy, Stephen Lewis said that Jack was "cruelly gone," taken from the world by a pernicious cancer at the pinnacle of his career; but who knows the back-story to Jack's early demise? Jack Layton had his own karma to work off, and "old whore life" snatched his physical life for spiritual recompense to bring him one step closer to spiritual wholeness; but one thing is certain of Jack's "cruel" death, and that is this: he died with grace.

Grace was Jack Layton's legacy to the world. He knew in his heart that the way of Grace was the path to spiritual wholeness, and that the way of Grace was the way of service; this is why he dedicated his life to serving his fellow Canadians, and serve he did as so many mourners attested as they told their stories of how Jack had touched their lives.

The way of Grace is the way of love, and love cares. Love "spends itself willingly (and wisely) for others," said the Monks of New Skete in their inspiring little book *In the Spirit of Happiness,* "be it with time, attention, money, or simply concern," and Jack was known for the time he spent with his constituents. He was a great listener, because he cared; and he acted upon his fellow Canadian's concerns, especially minority groups.

One of the most obvious faces of love is generosity, and Jack Layton was generous with his time for people. Saturday evening, the day of Jack's funeral, a neighbor dropped by our house with a bottle of wine. She had a trying day at her cottage here in Georgian Bay working with the electrician, and she wanted to unwind; so she and Penny sat for an hour or so sipping wine and talking, and she shared a very touching story about Jack Layton that captures the essence of the way of Grace that defined Jack's life.

She told Penny that her mother had an elderly friend that lived in Jack's riding. This woman was having trouble with her taxes one year. The government had sent her forms and letters and she couldn't make heads or tails of them, and she didn't know where to turn; so she called up Jack Layton. Jack went over to her house and spent several hours going through her tax papers until it was all cleared up. Jack cared for people, and he served his fellow Canadians with his time, attention, and concern, which is why there was such an outpouring of love, affection, and heartfelt sorrow at his funeral service Saturday.

The way of love makes us whole, and Jack Layton knew that serving his fellow man was an act of worship because there can be no greater act of worship than serving life. This is why Stephen Lewis called Jack "a lovely, lovely man," and why Jack, who could have raged at the "old whore" for taking his life so "cruelly", wrote in his last letter to the people of Canada: ***My friends, love is better than anger…***

23. Old Whore Life

I began this second volume of spiritual musings with the intention of exploring the concept of "old whore life." This image of life being like an "old whore" that screws us of our virtue came to me when I was in the throes of "working" on myself with Gurdjieff's powerful teaching of self-transformation, which I came to realize is the essential dynamic of all spiritual paths, only Gurdjieff spelled it out much more clearly for me.

With his teaching we could complete what Nature could not do for us and realize our immortal spiritual nature. According to Gurdjieff, Nature could only evolve us so far and no further, and to continue evolution we had to transform our consciousness by "working" on ourselves. We did this by practicing certain techniques like *voluntary effort, conscious suffering, self-remembering*, and *non-identification*.

These techniques became increasingly more difficult the more one realized how they worked, because as one transformed one's consciousness one stirred up the negative energies of one's life (and life at large) that did not want to be transformed. This is where I caught my first glimpse of "old whore life," but I will explain later how I "saw" her.

"Old whore life" is my metaphor for the negative energies of life, but "old whore life" is more than a metaphor. "Old whore life" is also a psychic entity. This may be hard to swallow, but in light of Carl Jung's understanding of what the devil is in the context of his psychology (he called the devil the Archetypal Shadow), it's not far-fetched to call "old whore life" a psychic entity. Actually "old whore life" is Jung's Archetypal Shadow Self—the collective consciousnesses of all the shadow selves of the world, and by shadow self Jung meant the repressed side of our personality.

So "old whore life" is both metaphor and psychic reality; but to catch the devil by the tail, if I may use that expression, I had to be very creative. In other words, to conceptualize "old whore life" I had to stand apart from myself, which was not easy to do. As Jung said, it takes great moral courage to see the shadow. This is why we seldom see "old whore life" despite the devastating effect she can have upon our life.

But still it's impossible to understand the concept of "old whore life" unless we understand that the purpose of life is to grow, evolve, and realize our spiritual nature. The problem with this is that we can only evolve so much in the natural process of evolution; this is why it is impossible to see "old whore life" at work in our life.

We can all feel the effects of "old whore life," like hurricane Irene that has just blown up the east coast of the States and Canada causing all kinds of devastation, or the foul little tempest that blew into my life two months ago, which started with accidentally biting into a cherry pit that cracked my tooth that had to be extracted; but just because we feel the effect of "old whore life" does not mean we know the cause.

"Old whore life" has many faces, and she can appear anytime, anywhere; and her sole purpose is to WAKE us up to our purpose in life—which is to grow in consciousness until we realize that we are responsible for the life we live.

This means quite simply that "old whore life" is not a psychic entity that exists independent of us, but a psychic entity that we create by how we live our life (*"Nature patterns after man, not man after nature,"* said Phylos the Tibetan); and the more we live by values that are inherently non self-transcending, the more we nourish the spirit of "old whore life." And by non self-transcending values, I mean values that break the spiritual laws of life—like the Spiritual Law of Non-interference.

This is a difficult law to discern, but I caught this law in my first volume of spiritual musings when I told the story of how I flashed my headlights at an oncoming police cruiser to warn the driver of a speed trap ahead. I didn't know it was a police cruiser, and he pulled me over for flashing my lights. This experience WOKE me up to the Law of Non-interference, because I had no right to interfere in another person's karma.

If that person coming down the highway was speeding, he was breaking the law and he was responsible for the consequences—which would be a fine for speeding. It was his karma, and I had no right to interfere in his karma by flashing him my lights to warn him of the speed trap ahead, because karma is an individual choice.

I got a speeding ticket driving back from Winnipeg one summer. I had gone to visit my sister, and on the way back I was driving my new little sports car at speeds well beyond the speed limit; but I was given a sign to slow down when I spotted a turtle crossing the highway. I stopped and placed the turtle on the other side of the road, but I failed to realize that the omniscient guiding force of life had "placed" that turtle in my path so I could slow down and avoid getting a speeding ticket!

OLD WHORE LIFE

I was too caught up in my new little sports car to pay attention to the language of life, and I got caught for speeding, and I cursed "old whore life" for the fine and loss of points on my driver's license. I blamed my speeding ticket on bad luck, but it wasn't bad luck; it was my own stupidity—*which the "old whore" woke me up to!*

But the problem people have is that they don't want to accept responsibility for their own ignorance or stupidity. It's easier to blame someone else or bad luck; never ourselves for what goes wrong in our life, and so we fail to connect the dots and get angry at life.

After years of trying to make sense of how life works I finally came to see that unless we see our life in the context of the Divine Plan of God—which is to grow in consciousness until we become spiritually self-realized beings—we will never make sense of the human condition, which is subject to such complexity that all the academic disciplines in the world put together can't make sense of it. As Gurdjieff would say, all this mental knowledge is "pouring from the empty into the void."

In other words we cannot make sense of life without including the spiritual dimension of life—meaning, our immortal spiritual self. We are Soul, and our purpose in life is to individuate the consciousness of Soul until we become spiritually self-realized beings; but to individuate our consciousness and realize our spiritual self we have to take evolution into our own hands, and this people refuse to do because it means taking responsibility for the life we live. We can't blame "old whore life" anymore.

We created the circumstances of our life by our own karma, and the only way we can change our life is by transcending ourselves; but to do that we have to live by values that are inherently self-transcending—values that create good karma, like kindness, compassion, forgiveness, honesty, truthfulness, charity, love, and fairness.

But we still have to be on guard for "old whore life," because the more we live by these higher values the more we threaten the hold she has on us, and she will come back at us with a vengeance to keep us trapped in the cycle of karma and reincarnation. This is the side of "old whore life" that few people want to see, because it's so far outside the box of conventional thought that it would shock the psyche to reveal it.

This is why my spiritual musings affect some of my readers the way they do. An old high school acquaintance responded to my musings blog on Facebook with this comment: "I'm tired of reading how good and smart he is. Puke puke!" She was threatened by my musings because they woke her up to her inherent responsibility to take evolution into her own hands and realize her spiritual purpose in life.

In effect, "old whore life" doesn't want her or anyone else to wake up, and so she mocked me for being so good and smart that it made her want to puke; but to take evolution into our own hands we have to be good and smart, because this is the only way we can ever break free of the hold that "old whore life" has on us.

It took a long time to realize that we ourselves are "old whore life," but once I caught a glimpse of the Archetypal Shadow I began to "work" on myself with the passion of a man possessed until I finally made the break and realized my true self.

But as long as we're in this world we will never really be free of "old whore life," so she's not through with me yet. I still have karma that needs to be resolved before I shuffle off this mortal coil, and I can only hope that she gives me a break for a while because I need a rest from the last foul wind that blew into my life.

If I may now, I'd like to explain how I caught my first glimpse of "old whore life," which came as a complete surprise to me....

I started practicing Gurdjieff's teaching while I was still at university, but I could not get a fix on what it meant to "work on oneself" and I hit a brick wall. One weekend I drove home to visit my parents and went for a long walk down the railroad tracks behind our house, to the lagoon and "little black bridge" and down to the breakwater and little man-made island and I sat on a rock and pondered my situation, which looked very bleak.

I had gone to university to find an answer to the most haunting question of my life, which came to me in a dream while I was living in France. I left my body in my dream and entered into the mind of every person in the world, and I took every question that every person in the world had ever asked and reduced them all to one question: *why am I?*

When I returned to Canada I went to university to find an answer to this question, but by my second year I began to doubt that philosophy would give me the answer, and during the first term of my third year I felt like I had been cast adrift in an endless sea of philosophical speculation, and I began to panic.

I had found Gurdjieff by pure "coincidence" when a fellow student gave me the gift of P. D. Ouspensky's book *In Search of the Miraculous, Fragments of an Unknown Teaching* (which was all about Gurdjieff's teaching), and I began to practice the techniques of self-transformation; but I could not penetrate the central mystery of his teaching, which he called "work on oneself." I simply could not grasp this concept!

As I walked the breakwater back to the mainland my steps were burdened with such heavy thought it felt like I left imprints on the rocks; and then for some reason known only to God I stopped and stared at the Nipigon River flowing past me on its way to Lake Superior and Ecclesiastes came to mind: *"All the rivers run into the sea; yet the sea is not full. Unto the place from whence the rivers come, thither they return again."*

I knew this was a reference to reincarnation, but that wasn't why those words came to my mind; they popped into my mind to inspire my *Royal Dictum*, which came to me after I looked up into the heavens and asked God what price I had to pay for truth, because I knew that nothing came for nothing. I stared at the river, and the thought came to me that to find my true self I had to go upstream to the headwaters of my life; but how?

Sophocles' play *Oedipus Rex* came to mind, and I thought of the terrible price that he had to pay for murdering his father and defiling his mother's bed. Oedipus banished himself out of his own kingdom for his crime against nature, and instantly I knew what price I had to pay for the truth I sought: I had to banish myself out of my own kingdom of the senses, and the words to my *Royal Dictum* came to me ready-made: *"I am like Oedipus Rex. I am going to exile myself out of my own kingdom. I embrace my becoming blindly, and I leave all of my sins behind me. I am going to go against the natural course of evolution and each obstacle that I encounter I will consume."*

And from the moment I stepped off the breakwater onto the mainland I began to live my life of exile like Oedipus Rex—no more pleasures of any kind, a personal edict of self-denial that I vowed to live for the rest of my life because in my heart I knew that this was the price I had to pay for the truth I sought!

Once I began living my *Royal Dictum* Gurdjieff's technique of *non-identification* began to make sense to me, and I experienced the benefits within days. I fueled Gurdjieff's teaching of "work on oneself" with my *Royal Dictum* for three and a half years and broke the hold that "old whore life" (my shadow) had upon me, and I gave "birth" to my spiritual self in my mother's kitchen one day while she was kneading bread dough on the kitchen table—meaning, I shifted my center of gravity from my ego to my spiritual self, and from that moment on I have never doubted my immortal nature.

Having found my true self, it was time to move on with my life; and as inspiration would have it the words of Ecclesiastes came to me one night to free me of the vow I had taken for life: *"Of making many books there is no end; and much study is a weariness of the flesh. Let us hear the conclusion of the whole matter: Fear God, and keep his commandments, for this is the whole duty of man. For God shall bring every work into judgment, with every secret thing, whether it be good, or whether it be evil"* (Eccl. 12: 12-14). After reading these words I went out to the Nipigon Inn Hotel for a drink and met a young lady whom I brought home, and it was sheer heaven having sex again!

Gurdjieff's teaching had served its purpose, and I had to find another path more suited to my new state of consciousness; and as "coincidence" would have it, once again my new path came right to me when a distant cousin unexpectedly visited my mother and introduced me to the Way of the Eternal, which I've been living ever since.

And now I can explain how I came to "see" the metaphysical nature of the transformative process of "working" on oneself, and why "old whore life" will do anything she can to screw us of our virtue…

The best point of entry that I can think of to explain the mystery of taking evolution into our own hands comes from Plato's dialogues. Socrates expounds upon the secret teaching of spiritual self-realization consciousness in Plato's *Phaedo*: *"And what is purification but the separation of the soul from the body, as I was saying before; the habit of soul gathering and collecting herself into herself, out of all the courses of the body; the dwelling in her own place alone, as in another life, so also in this, as far as she can, the release of the soul from the chains of the body?"*

The central principle of the Way is that soul, the spark of divine consciousness that we are all born with, evolves through the natural process of evolution until Nature can evolve soul no further; and to continue evolving we have to take evolution into our own hands, which Socrates taught in his philosophy of "gathering and collecting" soul into herself. But why, one may ask, cannot Nature evolve soul any further?

The purpose of natural evolution is to individuate the life force, which is the consciousness of life; and once Nature has evolved soul to the point where it becomes aware of itself—as I experienced in my past-life regression when I gave birth to my self-consciousness in my first primordial human lifetime—nature will evolve us through the process of karmic reconciliation; and by this I mean that the choices we make as a self-realized soul create personal karma, and from life to life we create and resolve personal karma. This is how we grow in self-consciousness in the cycle of life and death; but Nature cannot break the cycle of life and death for us. This we have to do ourselves, because Nature IS the cycle of life and death!

As simple as it may be, Nature would be going against itself to break the cycle of life and death; this is why Nature resists every effort we make to break the cycle. Socrates tells us that *"there is a doctrine uttered in secret that man is a prisoner who has no right to open the door of his prison and run away."* This prison is the recurring cycle of life and death, and the only way to break out is by "gathering and collecting" soul into herself—which I did by living Gurdjieff's teaching, my *Royal Dictum,* and the sayings of Jesus.

I grew so much in spiritual self-realization consciousness as I lived my eclectic spiritual path that I gave "birth" to my spiritual self in my mother's kitchen one day while she was kneading bread dough on the kitchen table. In one sudden and inexplicable moment I shifted my center of gravity from my human self-consciousness to my spiritual self-consciousness, and I knew that I was immortal. I could not explain the feeling that I experienced, but I just *knew* that I was Soul—my true, spiritual self!

In Christ's words, I gave spiritual birth to my life by "dying" to my life to "save" my life. I broke out of Nature's prison, but it cost me. As St. Paul would say, I was bought with a price; and the price I paid was my attachment to life.

This is the price that every soul has to pay to break out of Nature's prison, because our desire for life keeps us fettered to the endless cycle of karma and reincarnation; and unless we take the initiative and break this attachment we have to life we will remain prisoners to our own karma. Now, how does this relate to "old whore life"?

As strange as it may sound, "old whore life" is Nature's way of keeping soul attached to life. "Old whore life" will do everything she can to keep us creating karma that keeps us attached to life, and the moment we try to break our attachment to life—as I did with Gurdjieff's teaching, my *Royal Dictum,* and the sayings of Jesus—she will try to screw us of the virtue of our newly realized spiritual consciousness that we have "gathered and collected" through our efforts to break our attachment to life; and she screws us of our virtue by tempting us with every conceivable desire possible and frustrating every effort we make to garner spiritual consciousness by living a life of virtue!

This is the central mystery of spiritual self-realization consciousness—the spiritual energy ("virtue") that we garner as we live the Way; and by Way I mean the spiritual life. Socrates called it *purification,* Jesus called it *self-sacrifice*, Gurdjieff called it *"work on oneself,"* Buddhism called it *dying to the ego*; but by whatever name the Way is called, it is *the way of spiritual self-realization consciousness*, and it goes against Nature!

This is why the spiritual life is so hard to live, because it goes against the natural process of life and death; and it takes enormous commitment, courage, and wisdom to take evolution into our own hands. But we have no choice, because it is in our spiritual DNA to realize our true self, and from life to life we will return until we do.

So as much as I have grown to hate "old whore life" for her treacherous ways, I have to thank her for waking me up to my true self!

24. Stepping on Cracks

I went to a workshop on "Past Lives, Karma and Reincarnation" in Barrie last Sunday, but I drove into the city early and went to Georgian Mall first. I parked my car and walked to the main entrance, but as I walked the sidewalk I found myself paying attention to the cracks in the cement, and I chuckled as I consciously avoided stepping on them because of the old superstition that it's bad luck to step on cracks.

I thought about superstitions as I walked through the mall, making my way to Coles bookstore on the second floor where I browsed for half an hour or so to see if any book jumped out at me. None did, but one title teased my curiosity: THE BIG QUESTIONS, by Simon Blackburn, professor of philosophy at the University of Cambridge and "one of the most distinguished philosophers of our time."

I was a philosophy major at university. I studied philosophy because I thought that's where I would find the answer to my big question: *why am I?* But philosophy did not give me the answer. Philosophy simply introduced me to the world of the mind, and by my third year of studies I felt myself cast adrift in a sea of endless thought, and I just wanted to see if Simon Blackburn's book on the twenty big philosophical questions, starting with "Am I A Ghost In A Machine?" and ending with "Is Death To Be Feared?" would validate my suspicion that philosophy, for all of its brilliance, still cast one adrift in a sea of endless speculation—which, not to my surprise as I read selected chapters of the book when I got home after the workshop, it did; and I could not help but think of the thought-provoking saying from Blavatsky's little book *The Voice of Silence*: *"The Mind is the great Slayer of the Real. Let the disciple slay the Slayer."*

As I walked back to my car I consciously avoided stepping on the cement cracks, not because I believed that stepping on cracks would bring me bad luck, but because I wanted to dissipate myself of the consciousness that attracts bad luck by purposively not stepping on the cracks. This was my way of telling "old whore life" to get off my back!

"Old whore life" is the author of bad luck, and when she's around anything can go wrong, and often does. This is a mystery worthy of a spiritual musing…

The concept of "luck" has always intrigued me. Why are some people lucky and others unlucky? I can't tell you the number of times I've heard people say, "If there weren't two kinds of luck, I wouldn't have any." People sense luck, good and bad; and we would all like to know the magic formula for good luck because it would make life so much easier.

A woman I know very well goes to casinos regularly, and she wins much more often than not; but she seldom discloses her winnings. She learned that her unbelievable good luck made her family and friends jealous and resentful, so she stopped talking about her winnings. "That girl's got a horseshoe up her arse," her country born and bred father said to me one day over a cold beer. Her husband was an investment broker who died of a heart attack when he turned fifty and left her a million-dollar life insurance policy, plus an equal amount in investments; so it could be argued that her good luck at the casinos is confirmation of the law of attraction—i. e., much gathers more.

Out of curiosity, I asked her one day why she was so lucky at the casinos, and she replied: "I don't know. I just know that when I walk by a machine I know which one to play. I get a feeling, and I play the machine. I can tell when it stops being lucky, and I stop playing and walk around until another machine calls me to play."

"Amazing," I said, flabbergasted by her explanation; but the more I thought about it, the more it proved to me that luck is a matter of consciousness—which is why I avoided stepping on cement cracks, because I didn't want the consciousness of "old whore life" to attract bad luck into my life.

"For whosoever hath, to him shall be given, and he shall have more abundance," said Jesus, revealing the Spiritual Law of Attraction to his disciples; *"but whosoever hath not, from him shall be taken away even that he hath"* (Math. 13: 12).

What would an academic philosopher like the author of THE BIG QUESTIONS have to say about the spiritual law of like attracting like? I dread the thought! That's why I dropped out of university in my third year with Gurdjieff's teaching under my arm and went out into the real world to work out the answer to my big question; but that's a whole other musing. For now, I want to muse on luck and consciousness...

My father was unlucky. I knew my father well. He had a dark shadow; meaning, he was deeply influenced by the dark, repressed side of his personality. He had a dark shadow because he was so karmically unresolved; or, to express it differently, he had a lot of personal demons that came out when he drank. My father was also very superstitious. He would make the sign of the cross whenever he began a little carpentry project, fearing that the devil would interfere and make his project go wrong, and they often did go wrong; which is why his life was such a struggle. Nothing seemed to go right for him.

I connected with Gurdjieff's teaching, and I lived it with such passionate commitment that I began to awaken to the Word within. The Word within is the "water of everlasting life," as Jesus called it, or the River of God that flows through life as St. Padre Pio referred to it; but by whatever name it goes, it is the Way.

The Way is a difficult concept to grasp. It has to be experienced to be appreciated, and the only way to experience the Way is to live it. Living the Way is what the spiritual life is all about, regardless what spiritual path one is on. In fact, one does not even have to be on a spiritual path to live the Way. The Way is more of an attitude than anything else. It is an attitude of high-mindedness that opens one up to the Word.

The Word is the Voice of God, the consciousness of Holy Spirit, and when one is open to the Word God guides one's life. The more I "worked" on myself with Gurdjieff's teaching, the more I could "see" and "hear" the Word, which is why I gravitated to Christ's sayings. The sayings of Jesus are little gateways to salvation, or spiritual self-realization consciousness, and as I lived them I grew in spiritual consciousness so much that I began to "see" the shadow side of personality; and it wasn't long before I connected the dots and realized that our shadow is our unresolved karmic self, and it is the unresolved consciousness of our shadow self that we have to transform to realize our true self and be "saved." But what does all of this have to do with luck?

Everything. Luck is a matter of consciousness, and we determine the nature of our consciousness by how we live our life. When the disciples asked Jesus why he spoke to the public in parables, he replied that it was given to them to know the mysteries of the kingdom of heaven, but not to the public; and then he revealed the Law of Attraction: *"For whosoever hath, to him shall be given, and he shall have more abundance."*

Obviously the disciples had realized enough of the consciousness of the Word by how they had lived their life to be attracted to Jesus Christ, who was the Word incarnate; which is why he did not have to give them the Word in parable form as he did to the public. The disciples had enough of the consciousness of the Word to receive the Word in "more abundance," which they did through Jesus. In effect, the disciples were blessed with the Word and had the "good luck" to find Jesus Christ.

Jesus also said, *"Whosoever hath not, from him shall be taken away even that he hath."* This is the obverse side of the Law of Attraction. To simplify the Law of Attraction, one could say that much gathers more, and less gathers less; which means that the more one has of something, the more he will attract more of what he has into his life; and the less one has of something, the more he is likely to lose what he has because it will be pulled away from him by those who have more of what he has—hence the popular saying, the rich get richer and the poor get poorer. *This is the metaphysics of good and bad luck!*

The metaphysics of luck explains sayings like: nothing succeeds like success, it takes money to make money, birds of a feather flock together, misery loves company, it takes one to know one, and so on; all confirming the Law of Attraction. So why did I refuse to step on the cement cracks when I walked to the Georgian Mall entrance on Sunday?

I laughed when I caught myself not stepping on the cracks, because I knew about the Law of Attraction, and I used the superstition to remind myself that my own consciousness attracts more of its own kind, and I did not want to activate my own shadow which would only invite "old whore life," the author and principle agent of bad luck, into my life!

25. The Archetypal False Self of Man

I've grown tired of "old whore life." Honestly. And I can't wait to leave this world. Not that I have a death wish; I'm just tired of the whole process of life. And just what do I mean by the process of life? Let's make this today's spiritual musing…

I came into this world to find my way out of the process of life, so I had the innate knowledge that life is the means by which we grow in spiritual consciousness until we realize our divine essence. As spiritual beings, we all have this innate knowledge; but I awakened to it in my efforts to find my way out of the life process.

The vast majority of people are asleep to their spiritual purpose in life, which is to find the way out of the life process; and life after life they are reborn into the life process to experience more life and grow in spiritual consciousness until they too become so tired of the life process that they will want to leave this world, and they become seekers.

I became a seeker at a very early age, because I came into this world with a strong desire to find the way out of the life process; and I found the Way, which I have been living for the better part of my life now. That's why I'm so tired of "old whore life"—*because I am so acutely conscious of the life process!*

The life process is the never-ending play of karma. St. Padre Pio told me in one of my spiritual healing sessions that ***life is a journey of the self through vanity to humility***;

and believe me, this journey can get so fatiguing that you just want out of life.

As much as it hurts to say this, "old whore life" has worn me down, and all I want to do is rest, and rest, and rest—which is why I can't wait to leave this world. "Old whore life" is my own unresolved vanity, of course; but I am so tired of this journey to humility that I want out of the whole process, and my only consolation is that I know that I am "old whore life" and am responsible for my own life-fatigue.

"Know thyself" was the Delphic imperative that fueled my quest for my real self, but I had no idea what it meant to know myself. *"This above all, to thine own self be true,"* said Shakespeare, which has been quoted so often that one would think the meaning would be as obvious as the morning sun; but which self are we to be true to?

The most tragic person in the world is he who is true to his wrong self, because he is so blind to "old whore life" that he will never know that he is true to his false self!

When I was in high school I wrote a poem that shocked my English teacher, and all the teachers in the staff room that he read it to. It shocked me when I wrote it. Actually, I didn't write it; it poured out of me from God knows where. My *daemon*, probably.

My poem was called "Noman," and it told the story of how Noman was summoned to God for an accounting and condemned to the "fourth corner of the abyss" to find the lost soul of God—his own soul, which he had lost in the life process!

I was Noman. I was summoned to God in my poem, and I was condemned by God to the abyss to find my lost soul, and as I fell from heaven I shouted: —

"Open you vile, voracious, loveable sweet whore!
God, why hast thou forsaken me?"

I was angry at God for condemning me to the life process, and I embraced "old whore life." Like the Fallen Angel in John Milton's epic poem *Paradise Lost*, I too boasted in defiant rage at God: *"Better to reign in hell than serve in heaven!"*

But that was long ago, and I am tired of "old whore life" now. I am so tired of the never-ending strain of karmic reconciliation that it has fatigued my soul, and I want out of the life process; but I can't leave without making my peace with "old whore life."

That's why I went to a gifted Medical Intuitive for a spiritual healing last summer. I knew I had deep anger issues with God, but I could not resolve my anger until I became aware of my own vanity, which I could not do on my own. That's why the Ascended Master of Humility St. Padre Pio came to my aid. I don't know exactly how it happened, but his humility slew the beast of my vanity, and I am no longer angry at God.

This was such a powerful experience that it opened the door to another book with the Ascended Master after I publish *Healing with Padre Pio,* a book on Soul's journey through vanity to humility that is going to be drawn from the inspiration of Ecclesiastes: *"Vanity of vanities, saith the Preacher, vanity of vanities; all is vanity. What profit hath a man of all his labor which he taketh under the sun?"*

"Old whore life" seduced me and kept me blind to my own vanity, and life after life I returned to be played the fool until I could suffer myself no longer; that's why in my early twenties after I had an experience that shocked my conscience awake I sold my pool hall and vending machine business and went to France to begin my quest for my real self. Little did I realize however that my quest was Noman's quest for the lost soul of God!

It's taken a lifetime to come to the realization that Noman is "old whore life" and the archetypal false self of man; but that's my consolation now, knowing that we all have two selves, one false and one real. Noman is our false self, and Soul is our real self; and the only way to get from THERE to HERE is through "old whore life"!

26. Why Can't We Remember Our Past Lives?

Ever since I read Jess Stearn's book on Taylor Caldwell's past lives (*The Search for a Soul: Taylor Caldwell's Psychics Lives*) I wanted to write a book on my own past lives, which I finally did some twenty years later after I had seven past life regressions here in Georgian Bay; then one day I asked myself, why can't we remember our past lives?

We all have past lives. Just because we don't believe in reincarnation or remember our past lives does not mean we did not live before. Even Jesus Christ had past lives. He does not make much reference to reincarnation in his teaching, but it's there couched in his words. I asked St. Padre Pio about this, and he told me that Jesus had past lives—despite the shocking information that he gave me about Jesus coming from the future.

"A future presupposes a past," I said to the Good Saint, who was being channeled for my spiritual healing sessions by a very gifted woman, "so Jesus must have had previous lives; or did he come from another dimension?"

"Both," replied the Ascended Master.

There you have it, another mystery about Jesus Christ that the world knows nothing about. That was the first time I had heard that Jesus came from the future, but I could not explore it at the time because I wasn't ready to explore it. Perhaps in my next project with St. Padre Pio I will explore this new mystery about Jesus. For now I want to do a spiritual musing on why we cannot remember our past lives...

In all the spiritual books that I have read (and I've read too many to remember) the only answer I found to this question was that we're not allowed to remember our past lives until we are ready to deal with this knowledge; but what is it about this knowledge that we can't deal with? And what does it mean to be ready for this knowledge?

I was never able to figure this out until I had my regressions and worked out the Divine Plan of God. Once I connected the dots and caught a glimpse of the Divine Plan of God I began to see the logic behind the life process, and by life process I mean the recurring cycle of life and death that is governed by the Laws of Karma and Reincarnation.

I was very fortunate in my regressions to experience my life as a spiritual being in the Body of God before I began my cycle of life and death in the world; and I also experienced the birth of my reflective self-consciousness in my first primordial human life on Earth in the same past life regression. Without these two experiences I would never have worked out the Divine Plan of God; but just what is the Divine Plan of God?

Briefly stated, the Divine Plan of God has to do with expanding the consciousness of God through the life process. God sends its atoms (sparks of divine consciousness) into the lower worlds (the Physical, Astral, Causal, and Mental Planes) to evolve through the life process until we become spiritually self-realized, God conscious souls. We begin as embryonic souls that evolve through life, commencing in the lower life forms with no self-consciousness until we have realized enough consciousness to become aware of our own being, which I experienced in my first primordial human lifetime. Once we give birth to a reflective self-consciousness we create personal karma; and through the creation and resolution of personal karma we individuate the consciousness of life (the life force) until we are evolved enough to realize that we are spiritual beings who inhabit a physical body and that our purpose in life is total self-realization consciousness. But once we have evolved to the stage of self-realization consciousness through the natural process of karma and reincarnation we cannot evolve any further until we take evolution into our own hands, which we can only do by living the spiritual life consciously. That's the Divine Plan of God in a nutshell; but why aren't we allowed to remember our past lives?

Had I not experienced the disruptive effect that the consciousness of my past life regressions had upon my current life and my relationship with Penny, I would never have been able to solve the mystery of why we are not allowed to remember our past lives and what it means to be ready to deal with this knowledge.

I should mention that I was given glimpses of some of my past lives in my dreams before I became an active spiritual seeker. In my teens I had several past life recollection dreams that puzzled me. I knew that I lived in ancient Greece, and that I was a statesman in the city of Athens who rallied the men living in countryside to defend our beloved city that was under siege; and I knew that I was a black slave in southern Georgia who ran away from the plantation and got caught and whipped every Sunday morning to be made an example of to the other slaves; and I knew that I was a North American Indian who had to go through a very painful physical rite of passage to be initiated into manhood, not unlike the rite of passage that George Harris had to go through in the move *A Man Called Horse*.

These dreams were memories of some of my past lives, but I could not explain why I had awakened them until many years later when I was initiated into the mysteries of the secret teachings of the Way and learned that I was given these memories to fuel my quest for my true self; but who gave me these dreams?

The omniscient guiding force of life gave me these dreams, which in this case goes by the name of Dream Master. Divine Spirit is the Dream Master and the omniscient guiding force of life and it determines when we are ready to break out of the eternal cycle of life and death to complete our evolution to total self-realization consciousness.

Nature cannot evolve us any further than self-realization consciousness through the natural process of karma and reincarnation, of which we are not consciously aware; and we have to become aware of the life process to complete our destiny to spiritual self-realization and God consciousness, which is why we are given memories of some of our past lives in dreams to begin the second stage of our evolution through the life process.

In effect, we are not conscious of the first stage of evolution through life because we are unaware of how karma governs our evolution from one life to the next; but the more we evolve, the more conscious we become of how karma affects our life.

"What goes around comes around," says common wisdom, and once we have connected the dots enough to

realize that the energy we put out comes back to us in kind, which is a glimpse into how the karma works, the more conscious we become of the Law of Karma and the more we're allowed to remember our past lives because we can accept more responsibility for our own life.

It follows from this that we are not allowed to remember our past lives because it would only shock us to know that we are responsible for our own life. *"Why me, God?* we cry in despair, totally oblivious to the karma that we have created that has brought on our suffering; but it is through suffering that we grow in spiritual consciousness, because suffering burns off karma, and the more karma we burn off the more conscious we become of how the life process works. This is the mystery of the Divine Plan of God.

We're not allowed to remember our past lives then until we are spiritually mature enough to accept responsibility for our life. Knowledge of our past lives would only interfere in our spiritual growth, because it would affect our freedom of choice.

We have to be free to live our life in order to realize our spiritual destiny. Once I realized that we have two destinies—one karmic and personal, and one spiritual and divine—I connected the dots and saw how the life process worked.

Our karmic destiny is predetermined by our past life karma, and our spiritual DNA predetermines our divine destiny. We create the karma that determines the life we live, whether it is our current life or a future life; but whatever kind of life we live (writer, carpenter, nurse, or miner), we are all divinely driven to realize our spiritual destiny. And until we are evolved enough to accept responsibility for our spiritual evolution we will be governed by the natural process of karma and reincarnation until we are ready.

This is why we don't remember our past lives, because this knowledge would only interfere in our freedom to break our karmic bonds that keep us from realizing our spiritual destiny. In effect, we have to be free to transcend our life, and the memory of past lives would only interfere in our freedom to choose a different life.

This is difficult to grasp, and I would never have made sense of it without my seven past life regressions. Without this freedom to choose a new karmic course we would never break the pattern of our past lives; hence the reason Pythagoras told me in my Greek lifetime when I went to him in search of the secret knowledge that in order to realize my spiritual destiny I had to break the karmic pattern of my past lives, which was a pattern of lust for power.

In my regression I learned that Pythagoras taught me how to break my karmic lust for power (*by learning to serve instead of being served*), and as I lived the secret teaching that Pythagoras taught me I began a new karmic pattern that would allow me to align my personal destiny with my spiritual destiny, which I finally brought together into one destiny in my current lifetime with the Way that Gurdjieff's teaching opened up to me.

In effect I had to be free of the memory of my past lives to choose a life that would bring my personal destiny into alignment with my spiritual destiny, which isn't to say that we're not influenced by our past lives. We are, because our past life karma has a powerful, albeit unconscious influence upon the choices we make—which is why it is so hard to break old karmic patterns that keep us from realizing our spiritual destiny.

But the memory of our past lives would only make it that much more difficult to break the hold our past life karma has on us; that's why it is written in the Divine Plan of God that we are not allowed to remember our past lives until we are spiritually mature enough to not be overwhelmed by the consciousness of our past lives.

To make my point, I had a life in Paris in the 17th Century that was so sexually obsessed that when I went back to it in my regression I had to summon every ounce of moral strength to withstand the sexual consciousness of that lifetime, which I only managed to do because of my Gurdjieffian discipline; but I cannot imagine choosing to live Gurdjieff's teaching (and the sayings of Jesus) had I the memory of this debauched lifetime as I was growing up. I would have become a sexual addict, or God knows what; and I would never have had the freedom to choose a life that finally broke the karmic pattern of my sexually obsessed past life! That's why the Divine Plan of God does not allow us to remember our past lives, because we have to be free to choose a new life that permits us to realize our spiritual destiny of total self-realization consciousness.

27. Writing through the Hurt

In a letter to F. Scott Fitzgerald, the author of *The Great Gatsby* who introduced Hemingway to his gifted editor Maxwell Perkins, Ernest Hemingway, author of *The Old Man and the Sea* and winner of the Nobel Prize for literature wrote: "Forget your personal tragedy. We are all bitched from the start and you especially have to be hurt like hell before you can write seriously. But when you get the damned hurt use it—don't cheat with it. Be as faithful to it as a scientist—but don't think anything is of any importance because it happens to you or anyone belonging to you." (*Selected Letters,* 408)

There's an old saying that goes like this: *"You work hard and then you die."* This saying speaks to the struggles of life. It does not offer us much hope, which reminds me of a line from Margaret Atwood's poetry, "All we have is hope, but what hope is there?"

I can see the stark reality of these insights, but I don't agree with the pessimism of the struggles that we have to endure in life. Literature is all about man's struggle in life, which is simply referred to by writers as the human condition, and literature that offers us victory over man's struggle with "old whore life" fills our heart with joy—like Santiago's victory over the elements in Hemingway's novel *The Old Man and the Sea.*

Ascended Master St. Padre Pio told me—after his devastating humility slew my vanity in my spiritual healing sessions—that I would write more from the heart now, because my vanity kept me from the kind of empathy that every good writer has to have to write about the human condition, which is why I was so moved by an interview I read in the *Globe and Mail* with the former CBC Radio journalist and award-winning mystery writer Louise Penny who said, "I had to be hurt into writing." But because my heart was pried open with St. Padre Pio's healing grace does not mean that my newfound empathy for the human condition has obfuscated my vision of the stark realities of "old whore life." This is why I'm writing a book of spiritual musings on "old whore life"—to see if I can shed some light on our never-ending struggles in life.

Louise Penny did not begin her writing career until late in life. As she confessed in the interview: "You know, I tried. Every decade of my life I attempted to write a novel. But I had nothing to say. I was far too self-absorbed, and now I realize I was writing for others, so that they'd applaud me, see my genius, tell me how wonderful I am, or be jealous of my success…I had to be hurt into writing. I had to be wounded enough. Humbled enough. I had to learn compassion. Had to learn what it felt like to hate, and forgive, and to love and be loved. And to lose people close to me. Had to feel deep loneliness and sorrow. And then I could write" (*Globe and Mail*, Sept. 10/11). In effect, she had to experience the human condition before she could write effectively about life.

But it's one thing to empathize with the human condition and quite another to understand why we have to suffer the way we do, and if there's one thing that I've learned about human nature in my quest for my true self it's that people don't want to know about "old whore life" for fear of being found out for who they really are—which I learned ever so painfully with the angry response that I got from the people of my hometown to my novel *What Would I Say Today If I Were To Die Tomorrow?*

So how do I write about "old whore life" with an open and loving heart without shocking my reader with too much reality? That's my challenge, isn't it?

Ironically, I've always used my writing to process the soul-wrenching pain that I suffered in my quest for my true self—books that never got to see the light of day, like *Journey to Authenticity* and *Thoughts in Motion: Diary of a Holistic Runner*; but as honest as I was with myself, I was not as true as Hemingway when he told Fitzgerald that he had to be as true to his hurt as a scientist. I could never write through my hurt as the great writers have always done. Tolstoy said that he wrote his books with his life's blood, but I just couldn't go there. Why not?

I simply could not write though my hurt before my healing experience with St. Padre Pio, because it was too damn painful; but after he slew my vanity I had no reason not to. I did not have the courage to lay my soul bare of all of my humiliations, and I did everything possible to filter my life through all the intellectual energy that I could bring to bear, quoting writer after writer to mask the depths of my emotional pain; hence the beast of my vanity that took the devastating power of an Ascended Spiritual Master to slay.

I'm ready now to write the unfiltered story of how I was seduced by an offshoot Christian solar cult teaching that damaged my eyesight irreparably, and other humiliations like the real reason I sold my pool hall business and went to France, and why Penny and I relocated to Georgian Bay because my hometown turned against us because of my novel *What Would I Say Today If I Were To Die Tomorrow?* I will write through the hurt, because I have no reason not to now; but only when my Muse beckons…

28. Old Whore Life, *C'est Moi*

As I was trying to sleep last night I thought about "old whore life" and how difficult it is to acknowledge the reality of this concept. There's something disconcerting about the image of "old whore life" that keeps one at arm's length. This is obvious from the lukewarm response that I've been getting to my blog on my musings on "old whore life."

And yet, when we give "old whore life" another face—the face of cruelty, the face of rape, destructive rage, torture, brutal murder, and disgusting pornography, whatever evil man is capable of, it does not disconcert us because we are familiar with this kind of human depravity. But dare to call this evil an "old whore" that screws us of our virtue and people react in disbelief, as though this image has offended their sensibilities.

This puzzles me. It's as though people can accept the dark side of human nature as a given but cannot bring themselves to associate the sexual imagery of an old whore with the negative side of human nature, as though the image of life being like an old whore violates something personal, beautiful, and sacred about the feminine principle.

Sex is personal, beautiful, and sacred; but sexual consciousness can also be rapacious, vile, and profane; it all depends upon the individual. It has been said that offering the pleasures of sex for money is the oldest profession in the world, so why would the image of life being like an old whore that screws us of our virtue offend one's sensibilities?

I found this amusing as I tried to drift off to sleep. It was also frustrating, because I had failed to make my point about "old whore life." Then it occurred to me to approach it from another angle; from the angle of ordinary human behavior, like a boss trying to get the most out of his employees for the least amount of money; or the tradesman who cuts corners to maximize his profit; or the husband who controls his wife and family; or the woman who is having an affair with her best friend's husband; or professionals that gouge their clients because they can get away with it. This is the way of the world, isn't it?

I couldn't sleep, and I tossed and turned trying to understand why it was so difficult for people to see this kind of behavior as anything different from that of a rape—because that's what this kind of behavior is all about, raping another person of their virtue.

An employer who demands the most amount of work possible from his employees for the least amount of money is no different than a rapist who wants the pleasures of sex without paying for it, because the employer wants something for nothing. He wants free labor. So does the company that gouges its customers. So does the husband who forbids his wife to have her own life. He wants her all to himself. They all want something for nothing, and they're no different than rapists who want the pleasures of sex for nothing; so is it a stretch to see life as an "old whore" that screws us of our virtue?

Don't we all try to get something for nothing? Isn't this human nature? Or is it because I've connected this unconscionably selfish side of human behavior with the higher spiritual nature of man that has offended the reader's sensibilities?

This thought kept me from falling asleep. I put on a my ocean waves CD to lull myself to sleep, and before I drifted off I knew that I would have to do a spiritual musing on this concept of metaphorical rape, because I needed all the help I could get...

As I always do whenever I get an idea for a spiritual musing, I abandon to my Muse (my creative unconscious), which I did this morning, and the word KARMA popped into my mind; and I knew instantly that this was my entry point into my musing on metaphorical rape and why the image of "old whore life" offends my readers' sensibilities.

Karma is very personal. The energy that we put into life is responsible for the nature of our relationship with life. Karma is the cosmic law of cause and effect, which has been called the Law of Return. What goes around comes around, as the saying goes; so if we put out positive energy life is going to return positive energy back to us, and if we put out negative energy we can expect a negative return.

Karma is exact, absolutely impersonal, and it becomes part of our soul memory, so on a spiritual level we never forget what we have done. Karma may be exacted in our current lifetime, or in a future life; which means that we are not born with a clean slate. We are born with a karmic memory that determines the life we live. But we also have free will, so we can change our karmic fate. This is the mystery of our spiritual nature.

I puzzled for years about karma. It was merely a concept until I began to see how karma worked in life; and the more I connected the dots the more I discerned how karma balanced out the affairs of man, and the more responsibility I had to accept for my own behavior because

I began to see that I was responsible for whatever life threw my way, and I had to stop blaming God, as it were.

Before I realized that I was responsible for my own life I always blamed bad luck for my misfortunes, and out of my distemper was born the image of "old whore life" squatting obscenely upon my shoulders waiting for the next opportunity to screw me of my virtue; and it took years of living the conscious spiritual life of the Way before I realized the divine beauty of "old whore life," and by divine beauty I mean the reconciling grace of God—i.e., the merciful Law of Karma. It finally dawned on me that "old whore life" only screws us of our virtue to pay back our karmic debt to life so we can be brought into agreement with ourselves because we are out of karmic balance with life.

When we take something from life without paying for it, we cheat life and incur a karmic debt with life, and in good time life will exact payment from us, like a bank calling in its loan. If we don't pay our loan, the bank will forfeit our assets. This forfeiture of our assets would be like "old whore life" screwing us of our virtue.

Our problem is that we don't realize that "old whore life" has a karmic right to screw us of our virtue, and we rant and rave at life's unfairness—which we can do from lifetime to lifetime, as I apparently did as I learned from my past-life regressions. But it doesn't do any good to rant and rave. "Old whore life" will continue to exact payment from us until we wake up and realize that *we screw ourselves of our own virtue every time we cheat life.*

"Old whore life," *c'est moi.* That's why this image offends the reader's sensibilities. Who wants to be seen as an "old whore" that screws himself of his own virtue?

This is why Carl Jung said that it takes great moral courage to see our shadow. The shadow is our dark side. It is our "old whore," and we will do everything we can to keep this side of our personality in the dark; so is it any wonder that one would be offended when their shadow is brought out into the light, as I have done with my musings?

29. Blowing the Whistle on Old Whore Life

Writers are whistle-blowers. Writers write to get to the truth of life. It doesn't matter whether one is a poet, a playwright, a mystery writer, a science fiction writer, a fantasy writer, or a writer of short stories or the literary novel that addresses the human condition; all creative writing seeks to get to the truth of life—ergo, writers are whistle-blowers. In a word, creative writing is "an act of the imagination that transforms reality into a greater perception of what is," to borrow a phrase from the American poet Adrienne Rich.

But there is whistle-blowing and there is whistle-blowing, and the difference in shade determines the success of the author (given his talent for story telling). One very successful writer (Truman Capote, I believe) attended a party in New York City, by invitation only, and the hostess praised him on the success of his latest novel. The people he wrote about were not the most savory people, and it intrigued her to know where he got his inspiration. "Where *do* you get your characters from?" asked the hostess, with bemused wonder.

He looked at her, then he gave a long slow glance around the room, and with a straight face said, "Right here, Mam; right here."

She did not identify with the people in his novel because she had a blind eye to the dark side of her own personality, so when he implied that he drew his inspiration from people like those at her party, which included her, she took offense.

The truth hurts when it hits close to home. This is why people both respect and hate whistle-blowers. They respect them when they tell the truth about others, but hate them when they tell the truth about them. This has always been the case, and I should've known this when I decided to blow the whistle on "old whore life" in my musings.

But I really had no choice. I spent my whole life questing for my true self, and in my quest I had to come to terms with my own dark side; and so successful did I become in my quest for my true self that I wrote in my journal, *"Satan, you are so crafty that I know not which is you and which is me."* Finally, I stood face to face with my own shadow.

And once I got a fix on the dark side of my own personality I began to get a fix on the dark side of life; and I began to see the "old whore" everywhere!

The "old whore" is the dark side of the human personality. She is our shadow self, and collectively she is "old whore life"—the Archetypal Shadow, to use Jung's term, or what religion has called Satan. And who wants to see the devil part of themselves?

"Hell is other people," said Sartre; but he had no idea how insightful he was in his observation. Other people certainly do constitute the consciousness that we call hell, but to other people we are also the other; so we are part of the same consciousness of life. And yet, we refuse to see ourselves in that light. This is why we stay trapped in our own ego and write brilliant plays like *No Exit*.

Ego is our mental self. Ego is the mental process that we use to experience life and grow in spiritual consciousness, but it is not our real self. Soul is our real self, and we will never find our true self until we break free of the hold that our ephemeral mental self has on us. But breaking the hold that ego has on us means that we have to become aware of the dark side of our personality, and to do this we have to confront our own shadow, which is why people resent anyone who blows the whistle on "old whore life."

Jesus blew the whistle on "old whore life." ***"Get thee behind me, Satan,"*** he said to his disciple Peter, who was trying to stop Jesus from his mission of liberating Soul from the limits of human consciousness—meaning, the ego.

Christ's mission was to introduce the Way to the world, and he told his disciples that he would endure much suffering and even be killed, but that he would be raised on the third day; and Peter tried to stop Jesus. If I may, let me quote the passage that puts Christ's teaching of salvation into a modern, comprehensible context: —

"From that time forth began Jesus to shew unto his disciples, how that he must go unto Jerusalem, and suffer many things of the elders and chief priests and scribes, and be killed, and be raised again the third day.

"Then Peter took him, and began to rebuke him, saying, Be it far from thee, Lord; this shall not be unto thee.

"But he turned, and said unto Peter, ***Get thee behind me, Satan: thou art an offense unto me: for thou savourest not the things that be of God, but those that be of men.***

"Then said Jesus unto his disciples, ***If any man will come after me, let him deny himself and take up his cross, and follow me.***

180

"For whosoever will save his life shall lose it: and whosoever will lose his life for my sake shall find it.

"For what is a man profited, if he shall gain the whole world, and lose his own soul? or what shall a man give in exchange for his soul?" (Math. 16: 21-26)

In this passage Jesus reveals the essential secret of the Way, which is the secret of liberating Soul from the consciousness of its human self; and the way to free Soul from its ego is by transforming our consciousness through self-sacrifice—i.e., the sacrifice of ego consciousness. And the way to sacrifice ego consciousness is by "dying" to the values that keep ego bound to the ways of the world—which is not easy to do, because "old whore life" (Satan) will do everything to keep ego from being sacrificed. That's why Jesus said *"many are called, but few are chosen."* One has to be ready to take evolution into his own hands.

I blew the whistle on "old whore life" with my novel *What Would I Say Today If I Were To Die Tomorrow?* I revealed the dark shadow personality of my hometown, but so shocked was my community that it turned on me like a dog that had been disturbed from its sleep. But I am not the only writer who has blown the whistle on their community.

When the short story writer Alice Munro was asked by Shelagh Rogers on a CBC Radio interview "What do the people of your hometown think of your stories?" she replied, "I don't know. They don't talk to me."

It takes courage to tell the truth about life, because "old whore life" does not want to be brought into the light of day. "Old whore life" is most herself when she is least discerned, and over the centuries she has become a master of deception; this is why it shocks people when "old whore life" is exposed where she is least expected to be found.

When Jesus addressed his disciple Peter by telling Satan to get behind him, he blew the whistle on "old whore life"—meaning, Peter's shadow self. Peter had no idea that Jesus was addressing his shadow, but Jesus went on to explain that to follow him one would have to take up their own cross and sacrifice their life (ego) to find their life (Soul).

Jesus spoke in code, but in light of today's psychology his message of salvation can be interpreted as a teaching for the transformation of consciousness. As one lives Christ's teaching, one transforms the consciousness of his lower self (ego) and realizes his higher self (Soul), which is the essential teaching of the Way; so is it any wonder that "old whore life" will do everything she can to keep writers from telling the truth about life?

Jesus said that the truth would make us free—*"If ye continue in my word, then are ye my disciples indeed. And ye shall know the truth, and the truth shall make you free"* (John 8: 31-32)—but freedom from what if not "old whore life"?

30. Falling in Love, or Falling in Karma?

This week I heard a variation of *"We don't choose love, love chooses us"* at least three or four times, the last time coming from Brad Pitt, one of my favorite actors (Penny and I saw his most recent movie *Moneyball* last night, which we both loved), who said in a TV interview, "We don't choose the ones we love" in reference to his mate Angelina Joli. I think my Muse wants me to do a spiritual musing on this concept…

Penny, my life companion for twenty-three years, keeps reminding me of something that I said to her when we first fell for each other: "I didn't choose you. You were chosen for me." *What a horrid thing to say to a woman!*

But I was so caught up in my own life at the time that I was insensitive to the effect I had on other people, and upon reflection I am horrified at how brutal I could be. No wonder I kept people at a distance. I didn't mean to. My spiritual guide even said to me in a dream one night, "Must you be so blunt?"

With characteristic arrogance, I replied, "I'm not blunt. I'm forthright."

Another Ascended Master said to me in another dream, "Must you always go for the jugular?" I didn't know what to reply, but I got the point.

But what does this have to with those we love? Maybe nothing, maybe everything; that's what I'm going to find out in this musing…

No one can define love, but we all know love when we experience it; and the more we experience love the more love we want because love satisfies that deep, inexplicable longing in our soul. That's the mystery of love.

Every spiritual path declares that God is love, as does everyone who has experienced the profound depths of love because in the experience of love one experiences a bliss so sweet and good and satisfying that one feels closer to God, which is why love is the essential teaching of all paths in life. But why is that? What is it about love that can satisfy man's hunger for meaning, purpose, personal relevance, and God?

People who love their work are on the path to wholeness, because their love nourishes that inexplicable longing in their soul which I learned in my quest for my true self is man's primary need for wholeness, and the more we grow in who we are the happier we will be because *the essential purpose of life is total self-realization consciousness.*

This is the mystery of the self, which is the central mystery of life; but to understand the mystery we have to understand the Divine Plan of God. John Keats in a letter to his brother ("The Vale of Soul Making") caught a glimpse of the Divine Plan of God. "There may be intelligences or sparks of divinity in millions," he writes, "but they are not Souls till they acquire identities, till each one is personally itself. Intelligences are atoms of perception—they know and they see and they are pure, in short, they are God. How then are Souls to be made? How then are these sparks which are God to have identity given unto them—so as to even possess a bliss peculiar to each one by individual existence?

How but by a medium of a world like this?" (*Values*, J. G. Bennett, 12)

Ancient wisdom confirms the poet's insight into the Divine Plan of God in the saying "life is a school for the soul," but if this is true (and all my experience leads me to conclude that it is), then who is our teacher?

Karma is our teacher. Karma is soul's relationship with life, and in our relationship with life we learn the lessons that we need to grow in our wholeness. Our relationship with life is very complicated, and it spans the centuries because it takes lifetimes to learn our karmic lessons; like the karmic lesson I had to learn with Penny.

Penny and I have a long karmic history. We've been together in many lifetimes, the most recent being in Genoa, Italy in the 18th Century. We were married. I was an enviably successful textile baron and man of the world. I dishonored my wife and family by leaving my wife for my mistress, and my karmic lesson with Penny was to reclaim the honor of our love. The only way I could do that was by choosing my love for her over the love I had for my mistress who to my astonishment came into my life when Penny and I relocated to Georgian Bay!

Karma, the merciless teacher of life, repeated the karmic love triangle of my past life, and I had to choose between my love for Penny over my inexplicable infatuation with my past-life mistress! I chose my love for Penny and reclaimed the honor that I had betrayed in our life in Genoa; but it cost me. The emotions of my past-life betrayal were awakened by one of my past-life regressions, and they were so raw that Penny nearly packed her bags to leave me; but she didn't, and I managed to resolve the karma that I had created with her.

I hurt Penny in that life. I hurt her so deeply that I turned her heart to stone and she became a virtual recluse for the rest of her life; and I would never grow in spiritual wholeness until I made it up to her, so on the Other Side we decided to meet again in this lifetime to resolve our karmic connection from our life together in Genoa.

This explains my inexplicable attraction for Penny when we first met, and why I said to her, "I didn't choose you. You were chosen for me." I had an intuitive awareness that we had come together to resolve our past-life karma; and it also explains my inexplicable infatuation with my past-life mistress when I met her here in Georgian Bay!

I could have repeated the love triangle of our past life together (and the pull to do so was unbelievably strong), but once I realized what was happening I chose to honor my love for Penny and fought the karmic impulse to repeat my affair!

So, do we fall in love or fall in karma when we meet someone we are so attracted to that we just have to have them? When I fell for Penny, who was married at the time, I couldn't understand my attraction for her; nor could I understand my infatuation for the woman I learned was my past-life mistress; but because I had embraced the conscious spiritual life of the Way I understood the karmic lesson I was given, and I chose not to repeat my karmic pattern of betrayal. I chose to honor love this time, not my own needs!

"Old whore life" came at me with a vengeance when I was confronted with my karmic lesson, and it cost me to get the "old whore" off my back. I had to fight off all of my past-life emotional attachment that I had for the woman I had abandoned my wife and family for in Genoa, which to my astonishment had been awakened during one of my past-life regressions, and it was hell to pay; but I suffered the anguish of karmic reconciliation and made it up to Penny, whose love I had cruelly betrayed in Genoa!

So, no; I did not fall in love again with Penny in this life, nor with my past-life mistress when my love for her was awakened by my regression; I fell in karma with them. But I can say with a clear conscience that I have fallen in love with Penny since, and I cannot begin to explain the joy of our relationship today as we grow old together in our wholeness. Do we choose the ones we love, then; or does karma choose them for us?

The answer: BOTH!

31. The Anonymous Face of Old Whore Life

Exploring the consciousness of "old whore life" has been hard on me, but I was compelled by my Muse to bring some measure of spiritual clarity to the life process; however I'm glad to say that I can feel my focus shifting from the karmic patterns of "old whore life" to the spiritually transcending patterns of what Wordsworth called the "Happy Warrior" consciousness, and I can't wait to begin my third series of spiritual musings.

Writing about "old whore life" concentrated my focus on the shadow side of life, that faceless dimension of human consciousness that has to be resolved in order for man to realize his true self and fulfill his spiritual destiny. I called this unresolved aspect of human consciousness "old whore life" because I wanted to give it a name to identify it.

In effect, "old whore life" is a literary amalgam of the psychological, philosophical, and spiritual perspectives on the dark side of human nature, which has throughout history been called evil. "Old whore life" is the archetypal shadow side of human nature, but it's much more than that, which is why I was compelled to explore it in my musings.

Evil is the opposite of good; but evil also serves its purpose in the Divine Plan of God, and I felt compelled to explore this purpose in my musings. It has not been easy to catch the devil by the tail, as it were; but the more I focused my attention on how the shadow side of karma manifests in our daily life, the more conscious I became of "old whore life." This is why it has been so hard on me—because what you focus will automatically be attracted into your life!

The more I focused on "old whore life" with each spiritual musing that I wrote as I explored the shadow side of karma, the more conscious I became of "old whore life"—like when you buy a new car and start seeing the same model everywhere! —and this had a devastating effect upon me: it put me into a state of inexplicable anger!

For the life of me, I could not figure out where all of my anger at life was coming from. At first I blamed Murphy's Law, which was responsible for many little things going wrong in my life, like biting into a cherry pit that cracked my tooth which had to be extracted, and I wasn't entirely wrong; but the more I thought about my anger at life, the more I saw that it was not born of any particular experience.

I was just angry at life, pure and simple; and I couldn't understand why until I realized that *anger is the anonymous face of "old whore life."*

I had become so conscious of "old whore life" that the consciousness of the "old whore" became my consciousness, and for over two months I was in such a state of life anger that I had trouble living with myself, and I had to find a solution.

I did not know where to turn; but realizing that I had to find a way out of my anger I planted the seed for my solution, and before long I got an insight into my problem: I received a comment from an anonymous reader to my "Where Does Your Treasure Lie?" musing on my blog that was so absurdly vicious in its attack on my literary integrity that it combusted into the realization that I had finally pushed "old whore life" into a corner with my musings on

189

the shadow side of karma, and I burst into laughter at the irony of the anonymous post because "old whore life" never wants to be identified!

The post accused me of plagiarism because I "stole" my thoughts from other writers! *"Get a life,"* the anonymous poster angrily vented.

"That's it," I said to Penny over coffee on the morning that I read the vicious attack on my literary integrity; "I finally forced the old whore to show her face with my last musing, and it's time to move on," and my Muse instantly shifted my focus to the Happy Warrior dynamic of spiritual growth and evolution.

"Are you not going to write any more musings on "old whore life"? Penny asked.

"I finally saw her face in that post this morning, and that's enough for me," I replied, with a sense of relief. "I've got ten more to write to complete my second volume of spiritual musings, but I'm only going to post six more on my blog. I've pissed off the old hag enough, and I don't want to attract too much more anger energy into my life with my insights on the shadow side of karma." I need the energy of goodness to overcome the despair of my anger at life, and I think I know where to go for my inspiration."

"Where?" Penny asked.

"Wordsworth's poem *Character of the Happy Warrior,*" I replied.

"I hope it works, because I don't like this side of you," Penny said.

"It will," I promised, and went to my bookshelf for my Wordsworth collection of selected poems so I could officially begin my new adventure into that state of consciousness which I knew would attract the consciousness of goodness into my life, and I read the poem and got the title for my third series of spiritual musings: *The Happy Warrior, And Other Spiritual Musings*—and, as the Law of Attraction would have it, within minutes I got an email from Amazon books promoting the new biography on the author of that inspiring little allegory *The Alchemist*—*Paulo Coelho, A Warrior's Life*!

"It's started already," I said to Penny, amused by the timely coincidence of the warrior theme being pulled into my creative field of consciousness so quickly.

I showered, got dressed, and drove to Chapters in Barrie and bought the biography, as well as Coelho's new novel *Aleph*, smiling to myself at how life works!

32. The Eleventh Commandment

When Moses walked down Mount Sinai with his tablet of the Ten Commandments, he heard the Voice of God speaking to him: "Moses, I have one more commandment for my people to ponder on their journey through life." And Moses turned his face back to the top of the mountain, and he saw the Eleventh Commandment written in letters of flaming fire in the cloudless, pale blue sky: THOU SHALT NOT SCREW THYSELF.

Yesterday afternoon I had to go to Home Depot in Midland to pick up another seven pails of drywall joint compound for the taping job that I contracted to do for a neighbor, a job that I underbid by half because I was too caught up in my own stupid sense of moral ethics to calculate a price that honestly reflected the amount of work involved; and, at the risk of making myself look foolish once again (God, I hate it when this happens!), I have to confess once more that I got screwed by "old whore life"!

One would've thought that by now I would be on to the "old whore," but there seems to be no end to how we can seduce ourselves by our own stupidity. This is why I came to the sad realization that **stupidity is not a gift of God; it is entirely man-made**—as the experience of today's spiritual musing so categorically confirms…

If I have any regrets in my life, it would be not having had a mentor growing up. I've had to blaze my own trail in everything that I have done, and blazing my own trail has cost me dearly—emotionally, physically, mentally, and financially. Spiritually, blazing my own trail has been immensely rewarding because it brought me tons of suffering, and suffering, as they say, is good for the soul. But why, one may properly ask?

Let's explore the spiritual benefits of suffering before I open myself up to the legitimate ridicule of my generous act of stupidity in my laughably low estimate for taping the drywall of the basement of the new house that I had taped four years ago.

In the simplest terms possible, suffering burns off karma. Karma is the consciousness that we create in our relationship with life that keeps us bound to the recurring cycle of life and death—or, reincarnation if you will. In effect, suffering is Nature's way of evolving man to higher states of consciousness. But as Gurdjieff said, Nature can only evolve us so far; and to realize our full potential as sparks of divine consciousness we have to take evolution into our own hands and resolve our shadow self; but that's another musing. Suffice now to say that on the whole suffering is for fools, and by fools I mean those who refuse to see how the Spiritual Law of Karma works in their life.

But I'm not blind to karma. How then could I let the "old whore" screw me of my virtue once more after all I have done to bring her into the clear light of spiritual understanding? How could I be so damn stupid?

GUILT, pure and simple; the guilt born of my vain sense of moral ethics that I created to blaze my own trail to my true self! The guilt of not living up to my ideal of personal excellence in my trade, which so clouded my judgment when I gave my estimate to tape the house in question that I cut my price low enough to assuage my guilt but which was so out of proportion to the amount of work involved that it did not hit me until I began taping the basement and realized just how stupid I was for giving them such a low price!

This sounds confusing, but it's not. It's just bad business practice. So if I may, let me explain how I broke the Eleventh Commandment and screwed myself one more time by letting my emotional sense of guilt cloud my better business judgment!

Four years ago I taped the main floor of this new house, but I gave the owners a low estimate just to get the job. I was still new to the area and building up my business, and I tried to get all the work I could get, so I often gave low prices just to get the jobs; but the drawback to this business strategy was that when I got too much work I had to scramble to get it all done in time, and this put me under pressure. And when I'm under the gun to finish a job so I can get to my next job in time, I don't give my work all the attention it deserves, and the quality of my work suffers as it did in this house in question. I only did about an eighty-five percent quality job, which left a skunk on my conscience.

Four years later they asked me to give them an estimate to tape the drywall that they hung themselves in their basement, and out of guilt for not doing my best work for them on the upstairs I gave them a ridiculously low estimate, and now I have to do twice the work for half the going rate—which was a very stupid business decision.

I gave them a price by square footage, dropping my price by fifteen cents a square foot; but I failed to take into account all of the extra work involved taping all the bulkheads, double seams because they had a nine foot ceiling and all the extra joints because they only used eight foot sheets of drywall instead of ten and twelve foot sheets, not to mention all the screws that I had to re-screw because they did not use a drywall gun to screw in the drywall, and all the gaps they left when they cut out holes for the lights switches and sockets, and the terrible job they did with all the metal corner beads that I had to re-screw. I never took all of this extra work and fifteen pails of extra joint compound into account, and my work was doubled. I failed to acknowledge all of this extra work because I was trying to assuage my guilt for not doing my best work upstairs when I taped their house the first time, and now I have to live with my decision.

But I learned a lesson I will never forget. As I worked this job I did everything in my power to keep an even temperament and not beat myself up over my stupidity, and never again to give an estimate without stepping back and considering everything. In short, I will never let the "old whore" seduce me again using my own guilt to "screw" me of the virtue of my labor—eighty percent quality job or not!

I will do my best work on any job that I get from now on, but I will also charge accordingly, and that's all I can ask of myself. So as painful as it was doing this taping job, I learned an invaluable lesson about "old whore life" that makes my point about her better than any other experience I have ever had—that we are the "old whore" that screws us of our own virtue; and to be free of her we have to wake up to our own stupidity and not break the Eleventh Commandment: *THOU SHALT NOT SCREW THYSELF!*

33. My Muse Beckons

I didn't expect to go to Chapters in Barrie on Sunday, but we ended up there by chance when we failed to find the Maple Drive and Essa Road intersection that would take us to Food Basics where Penny and I had planned to go grocery shopping. We knew how to get to Essa Road from Chapters, which would take us to Food Basics on Essa Road, but I felt a strong nudge to go to the bookstore first, and when my Muse beckons I listen.

But before I get to the spiritual musing that I felt inspired to write this morning—which, by providential design cloaked as chance was triggered by my visit to Chapters on Sunday—let me say a word on these mysterious nudges.

These inner nudges come from the omniscient guiding force of life, which is Divine Spirit. They're kind of like an inner GPS (global positioning system), only they guide us to where we need to be for reasons that we do not understand; but after we get there we see the wisdom of our inner nudges because we feel more in tune with ourselves and life.

Spirit knows what's best for us, and Sunday's inner nudge was Spirit's way of reconnecting me with my creative self because I haven't done any new writing for a while; I've been pouring my energies into editing my novels *Healing with Padre Pio* and *Jesus Wears Dockers*. The moment we walked into Chapters I felt such a strong pull to the magazine section that I knew my Muse wanted me to get material for my next spiritual musing; hence today's musing on the magical process of creative writing.

I've had this insight for a long time now, that the human experience is the entry point out of the spiritually stifling patterns of our life and ultimately freedom from the recurring cycle of life and death—or, karma and reincarnation if you will; and I've known for a long time also that the creative writer is aware of this mysterious gateway to the ground of all being (Soul), but my experience at Chapters on Sunday set free this insight, and I'm compelled by my Muse now to explore it in a musing.

It's paradoxical to call the gateway out of the recurring patterns of our life an "entry point," but ironically *the only way out of our life is through life*—which makes it both an entry and exit point. Robert Frost realized this magical process in poetry writing when he wrote "the only way out is through." He caught a glimpse of this mysterious gateway to the ground of our being, which all poets strive for. As Adrienne Rich said, *"Poetry is an act of the imagination transforming reality into a deeper perception of what is."*

This is what every writer strives for—*"a deeper perception of what is"*— i.e., the truth of life. And this was brought to my attention when I browsed the magazine section at Chapters because I was strongly nudged to purchase four literary magazines to firm up my connection with my Muse: *The New Yorker Magazine*, which had a new story by Alice Munroe, one of my favorite short story writers; *The Atlantic Magazine,* because it had an article on John Updike, whose writing I love despite how much he intimidates me; *Harper's Magazine,* because it had a new story by Joyce Carol Oates, another writer that I admire;

197

and *UTNE Reader*, for its essay "The Power of Poetry," book reviews, and insightful essays. And, to put icing on the cake, as Penny was paying for the magazines with my debit card I was nudged to browse through a box of discount books and spotted a book called *The Hemingway Patrols, Ernest Hemingway and His Hunt for U-boats,* by Terry Mort—which I also purchased because I had just finished reading the new Hemingway bio *Hemingway's Boat,* by Paul Henderson which I loved!

Strangely enough, the thought that went through my mind as I checked out these magazines was the realization that a writer is on a very special journey through life, a journey of discovery; and with every poem, story, novel, or play that he writes he seeks "a deeper perception of what is"—meaning, the ground of being, or truth of life.

Hemingway was obsessed with truth in his writing. He began every story with "one true sentence," and he built his story upon that truth. His one true sentence was an entry point into the essential truth of the story he was creating. "Good writing is true writing," said Hemingway. "If he is making a story up it will be true in proportion to the amount of knowledge of life that he has and how conscientious he is; so that when he makes something up it is as it would truly be" (*By-Line: Ernest Hemingway,* 215).

It was to Hemingway's nature to know the subject he wrote about. His subject was life, and he did everything to experience as much life as he could so he could have a first-hand knowledge of his subject—fishing, hunting, marriage (he was married four times), sex (he had numerous affairs), boxing, bullfighting, drinking, war correspondent, whatever grabbed his interest, especially writing stories which was his most satisfying love.

"The more Hemingway knew about a subject, the more he could write about it. And, ironically, the more he knew, the more he could leave out of his stories," says Terry Mort in *The Hemingway Patrols* (81), which reflects Hemingway's ice-berg theory of writing: "If a writer of prose knows enough about what he is writing about he can omit things that he knows and the reader, if the writer is writing truly enough, will have a feeling of those things as strongly as though the writer had stated them. The dignity of movement of an iceberg is due to only one-eighth of it being above water" (*Death in the Afternoon,* 192).

Hemingway's obsession with truth in writing was going through my mind as I browsed the magazines in Chapters, and I had the strongest nudge to buy literary magazines because I knew that *the deepest perceptions of the truth of life are found in the literature of life*—the human experience that writers write about; hence my reason for exploring the magical process of creative writing in my musing today.

Providence confirmed my nudge for going to Chapters to firm up my connection with my Muse, because just as we got home CBC's *Writers and Company* had just come on air and I went upstairs and listened to Eleanor Wachtel interview Francisco Goldman on his novel *Say Her Name,* which is the story of his love and marriage to his young wife who died in a freak accident body surfing in the Pacific Ocean in the second year of their marriage.

What fascinated me about Goldman was his confirmation of Hemingway's conviction that a writer has to use his imagination to get to the truth of life, or "deeper perception of what is," which Hemingway learned the hard way when he experimented with his literal novel *The Green*

Hills of Africa, the actual story of his hunting safari in Africa with his second wife Pauline Pfeiffer. This literal novel failed as a work of art, and Hemingway concluded that his book needed the magic ingredient of imagination to elevate it to a work of art—exactly what Goldman said about his novel *Say Her Name,* which was based upon his relationship with his wife: "I made things up in order to be able to tell the truth."

Goldman wrote a novel memoir to get to the truth of his love for his wife Aura Estrada, because he knew that only with the magical process of creative writing would he be able to enter the mystical gateway to the truth of his love for her. He needed the creative process of fiction to get to the emotional truth of his relationship with Aura, and his novel *Say Her Name* confirms the magical process of creative writing.

Oddly enough, I sought to get to the truth of my own life with my first two novel memoirs *What Would I Say Today If I Were To Die Tomorrow?* and *On The Wings of Habitat, A Volunteer's Story* which were published almost ten years ago!

That's why I was nudged to buy the literary magazines at Chapters, because my Muse wanted me to reconnect with the magical process of creative writing; but what does this have to do with my insight that the only way out of our life is through life?

You have to *live* your life to realize the purpose of your life; that's what I mean when I say that the only way out of our life is through life, because in the *living* one taps into the creative life force, which is the Holy Current of God that flows through life. This is why Jesus stressed that one had to "do" (*live*) his sayings to realize the spiritual reward of his sayings, which he called treasure in heaven. In the *living* we are rewarded with self-transcendence, or what Jesus called salvation.

This is all very metaphysical, but there is no other way to describe the fundamental process of life that gives us the energy to grow in self-realization consciousness and realize our spiritual purpose in life, and only by *living* life (I have italicized the word "living" because I want to stress that one has to engage with life to get the most out of life) can we effectively tap into the creative life force that will set us free from our life.

As Frost said, "the only way out is through," which he illustrated with his iconic poem *The Road Not Taken*… "Two roads diverged in a wood, and I—/ I took the one less traveled by, /And that has made all the difference."!

It's a perplexing paradox, but we have to *live* our life to be free of our life. That's what Frost did. He quit his dead-end job teaching school, sold his farm and moved his young family to England and wrote poetry, and that made all the difference. That's what my Muse was trying to tell me on Sunday—to engage in the magical process of creative writing and realize the spiritual purpose of my life!

34. A Train Called Discovery

"All Aboard!" the conductor hollered, and I stepped aboard the train that had just pulled into the station. I didn't even know I had gotten off the *Old Whore Express* until I heard the conductor shouting to climb aboard the new train that had pulled into the station of my life, but I gladly stepped aboard and made myself comfortable in one of the window seats so I could enjoy the view on my journey to the next station of my life...

"Life is a journey of the self," said St. Padre Pio, but over the course of my ten spiritual healing sessions with the Ascended Master last year I came to the realization that mine was a journey through vanity to humility, which was why I got off the *Old Whore Express* and boarded *Discovery.*

I have no idea where *Discovery* is going to take me, but I know in my heart that it's not going to be anything like my journey on *Old Whore Express.* I dreaded my journey on *Old Whore Express.* I never knew what kind of setback was waiting for me around the next bend, and I couldn't wait to get to the next station of my life; that's why Spirit, the omniscient guiding force of life, introduced me to St. Padre Pio last summer.

I needed a spiritual healing. I had brought too much karmic baggage on board *Old Whore Express,* and not until I got rid of some of my excess baggage would I be allowed to step off *Old Whore Express* and board *Discovery.*

I had an excessive amount of vanity and I would never get off *Old Whore Express* until I got rid of some of my baggage; but how? I didn't even know that I had all that vanity until I started my spiritual healing sessions with the Ascended Master—whom I now call the Patron Saint of Humility. If it wasn't for St. Padre Pio I'd still be shooting past the stations of my life on *Old Whore Express*!

For the past several weeks I have been strongly nudged to research Carl Jung's life on the Internet. I met Carl Jung in a dream a few years ago. He had read my unpublished book *The Way of Soul* on the Other Side and wanted to discuss the alpha and omega of the self with me, and we talked for hours in my dream; perhaps as long, if not longer than his legendary thirteen hour conversation with Sigmund Freud.

It was such a memorable dream that I made Carl Jung a central character in my novel *The Waking Dream*. But this novel is not published yet, and I'm glad it's not now because with my new research on Jung I can do him the justice he deserves; and I am strongly nudged to work on *The Waking Dream* and get it out as soon as possible.

Incidentally, I was supposed to start working on *The Waking Dream* with my new editor last year; but I asked my publisher who was also the editor-in-chief to release me of my contract because his strongly suggested changes would have seriously damaged the integrity of my story; so Penny and I are going to publish it through Internet publishing, as we've already done with my novel *Keeper of the Flame* and first volume of my spiritual musings, *Just Going With The Flow*.

A movie based on Jung's iconic relationship with Sigmund Freud has just been released. It's called *A Dangerous Method*, directed by David Cronenberg; and I find the coincidence of these three events—my unexpected research on Carl Jung, my strong desire to get *The Waking Dream* reworked and published, and the release of *A Dangerous Method*—a little bit spooky, as though Providence was choreographing this whole new matrix of creative thought to address a longsuffering social *dis-ease.*

But I'm not surprised, because the older I get and the more I experience the human condition the more conscious I am of how the omniscient guiding force of life gives the world what it needs when it needs it. St. Padre Pio calls this "divine timing."

He used this phrase in the context of my spiritual healing: I had to be in a place of understanding before I could heal my wounded soul of my spiritual *dis-ease,* like the alcoholic who has to admit that he has a drinking problem before he can be healed of his addiction. And to be in a place of understanding I had to dump the karmic baggage of my excess vanity that kept me from boarding *Discovery* at the next station of my life; but like the proud alcoholic I had to first acknowledge my excess vanity to be healed.

That's what St. Padre Pio helped me do last year. With infinite patience he shone a light into the dark corners of my unconscious until I saw the proud face of my shadow self and I wanted to throw up at the sight of my insufferable spiritual conceit. That's when I began to heal my soul of the vanity that kept me from getting off *Old Whore Express.*

The same can be said of the wounded soul of the world: it has to be in a place of understanding before it can be healed; and all these environmental and social upheavals around the world are breaking down the unyielding walls of humanity's overconfident ego and setting the conditions for the spiritually crippled soul of the world to be healed. This is the view that I see as *Discovery* takes me to the next station of my life…

35. The Thrill of Discovery

I was watching *Ted Talks* on TV yesterday afternoon when Penny joined me. James Cameron, the director of *Titanic* and *Avatar,* both movies that Penny and I enjoyed, was talking about how he became a movie director, focusing on his passionate curiosity (especially for deep sea diving which inspired the idea for his movie *Titanic*), when he made a comment that spoke to me—especially when Penny reinforced Cameron's comment that he made movies for "the thrill of discovery."

"That's why you write, for the thrill of discovery," Penny confirmed, and she was absolutely correct—because nothing thrills me more than when the creative juices excite my nerve endings with surprising new insights that come when I'm writing!

I've been niggardly in my creative writing this past month because I've been editing my novels *Jesus Wears Dockers: The Messiah Secret Revealed, St. Paul's Conceit,* and *Healing with Padre Pio.* I had a pressing urgency to edit my two novels on Christ's secret teaching, so the moment I finished my preliminary edits of *Healing with Padre Pio* so Penny could begin her edit, I jumped into my Jesus and St. Paul books; but I'm content with them enough now to let them sit for a few more months before I get back to them with fresh eyes, because my first priority is getting *Healing with Padre Pio* out by summer.

Now, the curious thing about getting back into the creative frame of mind is that Divine Providence has come to my aid—as it always does whenever I'm ready to do my

Muse's bidding. It happened quite by chance, as it always does whenever Providence decides to bestow another blessing upon us, but I did not recognize the Hand of God until this morning upon writing a letter for my blog-book *The River of God: Private Letters to Ascended Master St. Padre Pio.*

I started writing my letter to the Good Saint yesterday morning, but during the night we had freezing rain and a hydro line must have gone down in our area because our power went out in the middle of writing my letter; so Penny and I drove to Mountainview mall in Midland to do some shopping; she browsing the woman's stores, and I *Coles* bookstore.

I only buy books now that I'm nudged to buy, unless I'm doing research for a novel that I'm working on and buy books that I need for my work-in-progress (like all the Padre Pio books that I needed for my novel *Healing with Padre Pio*), and yesterday I was strongly nudged to buy *What the Dog Saw*, by Malcolm Gladwell.

I had seen this articulate young writer on TV a few years ago when he was interviewed for his book *Outliers* (this is a scientific term to describe phenomena that lie outside normal experience), and I made a mental note to buy his book. Despite his massive crop of curly hair that could easily lead one to believe he was affecting an image, Malcolm Gladwell came across with such unpretentious confidence that he engaged my interest immediately, but for one reason or another I never bought his book; and then I heard him talking about his book *Blink* (a book about rapid cognition) on the radio and made another note to buy his books, but I didn't. And then I read a review in the *Globe and Mail* of his book *The Tipping Point* and I thought for sure I would buy this one, but again I didn't.

I guess I wasn't' ready for his perspective, but now I am; and Providence led me to his books. I say books, plural; because yesterday when I was browsing through *Coles* I came upon a boxed set of three hardcover books at a thirty percent discount, but because the set was wrapped in cellophane I couldn't look at the books to see what they were about. Even with the discount I was hesitant to invest fifty dollars (we've had to restrict our budget since my bypass surgery), but the three titles spoke to me—and no wonder, because they were *Outliers, Blink,* and *The Tipping Point*!

But as much as the titles spoke to me, I didn't make the connection with the author I had seen on TV a few years ago; so I put the boxed set down and continued browsing. That's when I came upon *What the Dog Saw*, which I picked up and skim-read and realized that it was the same author of the boxed set of books. I was excited by *What the Dog Saw* and was about to go back for the box set of his other books when Penny came back from her browsing and I got sidetracked. I paid for *What the Dog Saw* and we went to *Food Basics* to do some shopping for New Year's dinner that Penny's going to prepare today. A friend from Toronto who owns a cottage here in Georgian Bay is coming for dinner.

When we got home I sat in my recliner in front of the fire and read my Saturday's *National Post* (I go to Conrad Black's column first, which he's currently writing from prison in Florida, because the man fascinates me), and after I read my paper I read the preface to *What the Dog Saw* and my heart skipped a beat because Malcolm Gladwell spoke to my literary imperative—*to write from the heart about life today!*

Gladwell's editor at the *New Yorker* magazine describes his writing as "a new genre of story, an idea-driven narrative that's focused on the everyday," which speaks directly to the kind of writing that I do, only I write in the genre of fiction and he writes in the carefully researched, creatively brilliant genre of journalism.

I also write idea-driven narrative-style essays for my spiritual musings books, one which was just published (*Just Going With The Flow*), and the second volume (*Old Whore Life*) which I'm currently working on; and tomorrow morning I'm going back to Coles to buy Gladwell's other three books—if they're still there, because it was the only boxed set left. I trust it will be, because Providence has deemed that I read them; and I'm absolutely thrilled by my discovery of this fascinating writer whom Newsweek chose for the "Top Ten New Thought Leaders of the Decade" in 2011!

36. Movie, Dinner, and a Ticket

I was excited by the trailer and reviews, so I asked Penny if she wanted to see the movie *Extremely Loud & Incredibly Close* which was playing in Barrie. I had been checking the listings every week hoping to see if they had brought *The Way* to Barrie yet, a moving father/son drama inspired by *el Camino de Santiago de Compostela,* the pilgrimage in northern Spain also known as The Way of St. James that was first brought to the world's attention by Paulo Coelho's book *The Pilgrimage,* and then made famous by Shirley MacLaine's captivating memoir *The Camino,* but it didn't look like it would be coming to Barrie and we would have to see it on DVD, and in the meantime I wanted to treat Penny to dinner and a movie but instead it turned out to be a movie, dinner, and a ticket…

I had read Shirley MacLaine's book *The Camino,* which I enjoyed immensely as I have all of her books because her life fascinates me (any seeker who has the courage to break free of the status quo and follow their bliss fascinates me), and I also read Paulo Coehlo's *The Pilgrimage* because I wanted to know the back story to his international bestselling novel *The Alchemist* that had piqued my curiosity, which is why I wanted to see the movie inspired by *el Camino de Santiago de Compostela,* and given the enticing trailer and wonderful reviews on the Internet (starring Martin Sheen, and written and directed by his son Emilio Esteves), I wanted to take Penny to see *The Way.*

Life is the Way, and the Camino is a metaphor for life; but one has to wake up to the Way to see that life is a pilgrimage to one's true self. A father who walked the Camino with his teenage daughter caught a glimpse of this mysterious path that Jesus called the Way, which he shared on Youtube. "Although you return to everyday life," he wrote, "the Camino exists every day and every night."

He also said, "It's the voyage that counts, not the destination." But not until one's heart has been pried open by the pilgrimage will one appreciate what this means, which the Camino has a miraculous way of doing for many pilgrims. As one woman said upon completing her journey to St. James Cathedral in Santiago, "All I have now is love. That's what I take back home with me."

The journey to love is long and arduous and painful, and whether we know it or not we are always on this journey because life is the Way, and the Way is the path to love; and if we don't open our hearts to love in this lifetime, we will just keep coming back until we do because this is the essential purpose of life.

The first words that Jesus spoke to Glenda Green, the author of *Love without End, Jesus Speaks*, when she painted his portrait were, ***"Glenda, love is who you are."*** In one of my spiritual healings sessions that became the basis of my novel *Healing with Padre Pio,* St. Padre Pio confirmed that we are all sparks of divine consciousness, and the purpose of life is to evolve and awaken to our divine nature, which is love. This is the message that came through loud and clear for me in the movie *Extremely Loud & Incredibly Close.*

Based on Jonathan Safran Foer's novel *Extremely Loud & Incredibly Close,* Oscar Schell, the nine year old narrator goes on a pilgrimage through New York City looking for what lockbox or door that the key he found in a blue vase in his father's closet would open. His father, Peter Schell, died in the twin towers tragedy the year before, and Oscar wants to solve this last "reconnaissance" mission that his father has left for him.

The key in the vase was contained in a small envelop with the name "Black" on it. That was Oscar's only clue to solving the mystery of the key, and Oscar, who is an exceptionally gifted and sensitive child, goes on a quest throughout the city for the right person called Black who might know something about the key.

After eight months of Saturdays questing for the right Black, his search takes him to William Black, the owner of the vase that Oscar's father had purchased for an anniversary gift for his wife, and Oscar's pilgrimage ends because William Black's father had left the key in the vase for him. The key opened a bank deposit box, but William did not know the key was in the vase when he sold it to Oscar's father at the estate sale of his deceased father's possessions. He only found out when he read the letter that his father had left him.

Oscar returned the key to William, and it seems his quest ends in disappointment; but his pilgrimage had not only brought him closer to his father and introduced him to his estranged grandfather, it brought him closer to his distant mother, not to mention all the people that he touched along the way with the love that he had for his father.

When William told Oscar that his father had left the key for him in the blue vase, Oscar was heartbroken but happy to have found its rightful owner, and when he returned the key to William I felt the deepest rush of emotion because it suddenly dawned upon me that the lock that special key opened was the lock of the heart, and with tears in my eyes I turned to Penny and whispered, *"Love. That's the purpose of life. To open our hearts to love."*

Oscar's pilgrimage opened my heart, and I couldn't get over the love that had been set free from that young boy's quest. I was still so full of emotion from the matinee movie and dinner that I never noticed I was speeding when I got caught doing 90 in a 60 K zone; but after I explained to the officer that I was still on a high from our movie and dinner he only fined me for doing fifteen kilometers over the limit, which cut my fine down from two hundred and twenty dollars to fifty-five, and no points off my driver's license. Otherwise I would have lost four points, which would have raised my insurance.

"Old whore life must have felt I was just a bit too happy, and she came out to put a damper on my day; but I should have known better. I'll just have to be more mindful of my heavy foot from now on," I said to Penny, who laughed and said to me, "I see a musing in this. How about, Movie, Dinner, and a Ticket?"

37. The Courage to Be Instinctive

"As each plant grows from a seed and becomes an oak tree, so man becomes what he is meant to be. He ought to get there, but most get stuck."

C. G. Jung

I was doing some research on Paulo Coelho on the Internet the other day and came across a documentary video of his train trip across Siberia which became the basis of his novel *Aleph*, which I read a few months ago, and something he said inspired me to do a spiritual musing on the courage to be instinctive.

Coelho said that whenever he feels stuck in his life, his instincts tell him it's time to go on a journey; that's how he got to write *The Pilgrimage* (he walked the *Camino de Santiago de Compostela*, which inspired his allegorical novel *The Alchemist*), his novel *The Valkryies* (he and his wife embarked on a forty-day quest into the dangerous Mojave Desert where they encountered the biker warrior women called the Valkryies), and his latest novel *Aleph* (inspired by his Transiberian journey); but does one have to go on a physical journey to break out of the life rut they have fallen into?

That's what Julia Roberts did in the movie *Eat Pray Love*, the movie based upon Elizabeth Gilbert's memoir by the same name. A married woman realizes how unhappy her marriage really is, and that her life needs to go in a different direction. After a painful divorce, she takes off on a round-the-world trip to "find herself."

Penny and I tried several times to catch this movie at the theater, but each time we went they had sold out, so we ended up seeing different movies; but the other day Penny came home with the DVD *Eat Pray Love* and yesterday we invited our neighbor and his wife to join us for the evening to watch Julia Roberts "find herself."

We all enjoyed the movie, because on some level we all identified with Julia Robert's predicament—and that's what getting stuck in a life rut is, a predicament. Julia got out of her predicament by divorcing her husband and going on a trip to Italy, India, and Bali to "find herself," and she does find some measure of happiness. But why was she in a predicament to begin with?

What was Paulo Coelho's predicament? What is anyone's predicament that can weigh so heavily upon one's conscience it can make cowards of us all?

It takes courage to break out of one's predicament, which Julia Roberts had to summon to get out of a marriage she had outgrown. But she was packing a lot of guilt for divorcing her husband, which Penny easily identified with because she was burdened for years with the guilt of divorcing her husband, and which I could identify with also for at least two breakups that I had with different women before I met Penny. But why do we have to feel guilty for having the courage of our instincts?

When I broke up with Mary, who had separated from her alcoholic husband, I knew by the seventh month that our relationship would never be large enough to contain me (I was a seeker, growing in leaps and bounds in my quest for my real self), and I had to have the courage of my instincts to do the right thing to "find myself."

I tried to be as honest and gentle as I could be, but all the same it hurt like hell to break up with Mary. I wrote her a letter explaining why it was best for us to break up, but I did not mail the letter to her; I brought it to her house. She went into the living room to read it, and after an allotted time came back into the kitchen, her face red and eyes swollen with tears, and I hugged her, cried with her, and thanked her for our relationship.

Mary was good for me, and I hope I was good for her; but I could see that our relationship would never grow large enough to contain me, so I made the difficult choice to break it off and move on with my life; and that sums up the essential factor of the predicament that everyone falls into at least several times in their life. But do we have the courage to deal with our predicament honestly, being fair to all the parties concerned? That's the fun part, and the material for all kinds of sad and happy stories; or, as the case may be, both sad and happy as *Eat Pray Love* proved to be.

I learned on Facebook the other day that another woman in my life had passed away from cancer and memories flooded my mind of our relationship. Debbie wanted me to marry her, but I wasn't ready for marriage; so she gave me an ultimatum, which she had every right to do. We broke up and she got a job transfer to southern Ontario, but two or three years later she came back up north to visit and I took her out for dinner to catch up on her life. She wanted us to get back together again, but I wasn't in that place yet where I could make that kind of commitment; so we parted once more, and she got on with her life, got married, had a family, and now has sadly passed on.

I felt guilty for breaking up with Debbie and Mary, but I knew in my heart that I wasn't in that place where I could make that kind of commitment; and it hurt like hell to break up. This, of course, begs the question: why get involved, then?

I can't speak for anyone else, but I got involved hoping that our relationship would have the room for us to grow mutually in our individual interests, but with both Debbie and Mary they weren't. With Penny I got very lucky. Our relationship gives us all the room we need to be ourselves because we share the same spiritual values.

Still, why the guilt when we have the courage of our instincts and break free of our predicament so we can become who we are meant to be? Julia Roberts stopped growing in her marriage, and she had to "find herself." She wasn't driven to find herself like I was, because I had made a career of questing for my real self; but all the same, one day she could no longer deny the fact that she was in a predicament and had to get out, so she divorced her husband and went on a world trip to get back in touch with herself.

"Finding oneself" is a euphemism for one's need to get out of one's unhappy state of consciousness. Julia Roberts was no longer happy in her marriage. She had lost touch with herself, and in Italy she began to get back in touch with her sensual self by giving way to the pleasure of eating that wonderful Italian food, which I'm intimately familiar with; and in India she got in touch with her inner self through prayer and meditation; and in Bali she got into touch with her whole self by having the courage to love

217

again—but only after she let go of all the guilt that she was packing for having the courage of her instincts.

Most people don't have the courage of their instincts. That's why Carl Jung, who analyzed thousands of patients in his lifetime, came to the conclusion that most people get stuck on their journey to what they are meant to be. But it's never too late.

As the man who walked the Camino with his teenage daughter said, "It's the voyage that counts, not the destination." Meaning, one doesn't have to go on a physical journey like taking a trip around the world or walk the Camino to change one's life; one can change one's life by changing one's attitude about life. And one changes one's attitude by changing one's values. But that's another musing, for another time.

38. Waking Up to My Own Ignorance

"The older I get, the more I realize that I don't know enough to entirely cover my little finger nail. There'd be room for more."

C. J. Jung

I've just had another awakening. I've had many awakenings in my life, but this one took me by surprise. I've heard many intelligent, knowledgeable people admit that the more they knew the more they realized how little they knew, and as much as I understood what they meant by this—because the more I learned the more I realized how much more there was to learn—yesterday I became acutely conscious of the abysmal depths of my own ignorance, and I felt so humbled that I wanted to throw up.

I hated myself for my pretense to knowledge, because the moment I became acutely conscious of my own ignorance I saw how shallow I really was; and in an instant I felt a total readjustment of attitude—from one of blind pride to one of conscious humility. This is one side of my "old whore" (my shadow) that I did not expect to see, but I did; and I have to do a spiritual musing to explore how I woke up to my own ignorance...

For the past several months I've been doing an awful lot of research on the Internet. It all started with a very strong nudge to dig deeper into Carl Jung's psychology of the self so I could flesh in his character for my novel *The*

Waking Dream, which led to a deeper look into Gnosticism and Alchemy, subjects that Carl Jung drew upon for his understanding of the psyche and the individuation process, and this brought me to Marion Woodman, a Jungian analyst whose book *Bone: Dying into Life* was practically handed to me personally by Providence when I was doing research for my novel *Healing with Padre Pio,* and Marion Woodman led me to a ten hour film on Dr. Marie-Louise von Franz—also a Jungian analyst who worked with Carl Jung in Switzerland (I was familiar with her work. She wrote Chapter 3, "The Process of Individuation" for Jung's book *Man and his Symbols*) —and the documentary film "The Way of the Dream," which I watched yesterday.

Introduced by Marion Woodman, in this film Dr. Marie-Louise von Franz has an in-depth conversation with Fraser Boa, Marion Woodman's brother who was also a Jungian analyst. It is an in-depth documentary on every aspect of dreaming from the Jungian perspective, and although I only watched the first two videos yesterday at some point while listening to Dr. von Franz I had my humbling awakening. It had been coming on for some time, but something she said tipped the balance and I fell off the lofty perch of my intellectual pride into the humiliating abyss of my own ignorance.

I pondered my awakening all night long and again this morning, and I believe I have found the answer; but it is rather personal…

My interest in Carl Jung goes back many years. I "found" Gurdjieff while studying philosophy at university and made his teaching of "work on oneself" the mainstay of my life when I left university to look for the Way in the marketplace as I worked my humble trade of house painting, and I naturally gravitated to Carl Jung's psychology of the self.

Gurdjieff's teaching awakened the Word in me (the water of everlasting life, as Jesus called it), which brought me to the sayings of Jesus that purported to grant one eternal life if one learned how to interpret them correctly (*"Whoever finds the interpretation of these sayings will not taste death,"* said Jesus in the *Gospel of Thomas*), which I learned to do; and I did experience my spiritual rebirth, or the consciousness of my own immortality if you will, one day in my mother's kitchen while she was kneading bread dough.

So I had found the Way, lived the Way, and found my real self—meaning, I became conscious of my inner self; and I grew in spiritual consciousness until I realized enough gravitas to attract the secret teachings of the Light and Sound of God into my life. Quite by chance, which I later realized was providential design cloaked as chance, a member of this spiritual teaching came to my house and introduced me to this path.

"Do you believe in reincarnation?" she asked me.

"Of course," I replied.

"I have a book you might be interested in," she said, which I picked up at her cottage that evening; and no sooner did I get into it and I shouted, *"I'm home!"*

I had found my path, which is known to the world as the Way of the Eternal, and I became an initiate of the teachings of spiritual self-realization and God-consciousness—once again, because I had lived this secret teaching in my past lifetime in ancient Greece as a student of Pythagoras, who also taught me the secret knowledge of dreams.

Once more I was introduced to the secret knowledge of dreams when I became an initiate of the Light and Sound of God shortly after reading this book, and for over thirty years I have been an initiate of the secret knowledge of the Soul; so I felt I had a "privileged" insight into the way of the dream. But did I, really?

I felt I did, and that was my spiritual conceit. But the more research I did on Jung and his teaching, the more I began to feel less comfortable in my "privileged" knowledge of dreams. And then I watched five hours of "The Way of the Dream" in which Dr. von Franz talks about the dynamics of the dreaming process with Fraser Boa—drawing upon thirty years of personal experience as a Jungian psychotherapist and over sixty-eight thousand dream interpretations—and my spiritual conceit was shattered like a broken mirror.

Her knowledge of the dynamics of dreaming was so informative that I could not help but be humbled by her insightful interpretation of dreams, and I experienced a paradigm shift from my "privileged" position on the secret spiritual knowledge of dreams to a very humble understanding of the mysteries and wonder of the dreaming process.

Dr. von Franz woke me up to my spiritual conceit. This conceit was the face of my "old whore" (my shadow) that I simply could not see. Dr. von Franz said that the shadow is like our own back. We cannot see our backside. We can only see it in a mirror, and she became the mirror that revealed the spiritual conceit of my "privileged" position.

When I became an initiate of the secret teachings of the Light and Sound of God, I knew I had found my spiritual path; but the more I grew in the Way of the Eternal, the more conceited I became in the certainty of my spirituality. Not that I wasn't certain in my spirituality before—having awakened to the Word and experiencing my spiritual rebirth, I had enough spiritual certainty to intimidate Satan himself—but in the teachings of the Light and Sound of God I had found "the most direct path to God," and that began to instill in me a feeling of being very special, chosen, and privileged.

This feeling of spiritual elitism wasn't restricted to me alone. I noticed that this feeling was like an insidious worm that had worked its way into the consciousness of everyone who became an initiate of the secret teachings of the Light and Sound of God (especially obvious in Higher Initiates who are dangerously close to becoming a spiritual cult unto themselves), very much like the menacing worm of spiritual conceit that works its way into the consciousness of every baptized Christian who is convinced in the dogmatic belief that Jesus Christ is the only begotten Son of God and only savior of the world.

Dreams however speak the truth of one's life in particular and the collective life of man in general, which is why I was so fascinated by Jung's psychology of dreams. But the secret spiritual knowledge of dreams that I studied in my path forever seemed to want to usurp the psychological understanding of dreams; and it wasn't until I saw the face of "old whore life" (the false face of the Archetypal Shadow) as I listened to Dr. von Franz expounding upon the way of the dream did I get to see my

223

own backside (again), and I had a spontaneous readjustment of attitude from one of spiritual elitism to humility.

It is one thing to know (comprehend) that Truth has many faces, but quite another to realize (apprehend) that every face reflects the same Truth. *"The only value any truth has is in the degree of its realization. Truth fully realized is spiritual consciousness,"* said the torchbearer of the Light and Sound of God; and as I watched "The Way of the Dream" (I watched the last five hours this morning) and listened to Dr. von Franz interpret and expound upon the meaning of dreams, I awakened to the understanding that a Jungian psychology of dreams magnificently amplified the secret spiritual knowledge of dreams that I studied as a Higher Initiate of the secret teachings of the Light and Sound of God.

As I awakened to this understanding, I had the dawning REALIZATION that Truth is one, and I experienced a new sense of freedom as "old whore life" lost its grip on me and showed me the insolent face of my spiritual ignorance!

39. The Way of Soul in the Strange, Strange World of Dreams

A few months before the renowned psychoanalyst Carl Gustav Jung died, he wrote to an English correspondent: *"I have failed in my foremost task to open people's eyes to the fact that man has a soul, that there is a buried treasure in the field..."*

I met C.G. Jung in a dream one night. He came to me because he wanted to talk about my book *The Way of Soul*. This book wasn't published yet. It wasn't even transcribed. I had only begun transcribing the first chapter, but I got pulled into other projects and never completed the transcription of my remaining tapes, which would then have to be reworked and edited for publication; this is why I was so shocked when Jung held my book *The Way of Soul* in his hand and told me that he wanted to discuss it with me.

How I came to create *The Way of Soul* is a story in itself, which I have to relate to give context to my remarkable dream experience with Carl Jung. My spiritual musing today then is going to be on the way of Soul in the strange, strange world of dreams…

When I met Kevin Archer (the fictional name for the real life water color artist in my novel *The Waking Dream*) in the art gallery in Kildair (also a fictional name) in South Central Ontario, I was still processing all of the archetypal energy from the seven past-life regressions that I had just completed a month or so earlier.

In my fourth past-life regression I was brought back to the Great Ocean of Love and Mercy, which is the Body of God, where all atoms of God come from; and in the same regression I was brought back to my first primordial human life on earth when I experienced the birth of my reflective self-consciousness. I had such an explosion of consciousness because of my seven past-life regressions that I had to do something with all that archetypal energy, so I decided to do what I came to call a series of "Soul talk" books.

I decided to *let go and let Soul speak,* as it were (a technique somewhat akin to Jung's technique of *active imagination*), which became the inspiration for my three "Soul talk" books, starting with *The Way of Soul.* Every morning when I commuted to and from my work as a drywall taping and painting contractor I would talk into my mini recorder that I had hanging from my rear-view mirror, but I would not have done my three "Soul talk" books had I not met by pure "coincidence" Kevin Archer who had come to a depressing creative impasse in his art.

Providence brought us together. I need not expand upon this now because I have done so in *The Waking Dream* that was subsequently inspired by my three "soul talk" books; suffice to say that Kevin was ready to meet his new teacher, true to the old saying that when the student is ready a teacher appears, and out of my mouth poured all the inspiration that he needed to break through his impasse and continue on his artist's way to wholeness.

I didn't know that I was the teacher he was providentially designed to meet, because I never saw myself as a teacher (my personal motto was: *let the world find its own way*); but I could not get over how quickly and easily it was for Soul to speak whenever I met him. It was like every time we met he had pressing questions that needed answers, and the answers just poured out of me like Christ's "water of everlasting life." *It was bizarre!*

I live by the principle that the more we give to life, the more we will get from life, which applies to everything that we do in life, and I shared with Kevin whatever wisdom I had garnered about the creative process from all my years of spiritual questing; and in some strange and mystical way we connected on a Soul level that opened the "tap" in me and there was no stopping the wisdom that flowed from my higher self, so Kevin got all the answers that he needed whenever *I let go and let Soul speak...*

Soul is the Consciousness of God, and as atoms of God our journey through life is to become aware of our divine nature; and the omniscient guiding force of life, which has been called Divine Spirit, the Way, the Word, Logos, Grace, Tao, Chi, Baraka, *élan vital* and many other names, is the Voice of God that guides us to our higher self by signs, symbols, coincidences, and whatever means necessary—like meeting someone who points us in the right direction just as Kevin Archer and I met in the new art gallery of Kildair!

Jesus called the Way the "water of everlasting life," which he said was in every person, and if we could tap into this "water of everlasting life" we would find our way and realize our divine nature. With Gurdjieff's remarkable teaching of "work on oneself," I learned how to tap into this spiritually quenching "water of everlasting life."

Actually, one cannot learn how to do this, as such; one can only realize it by *doing*, as Jesus said. In other words, one has to *live* the Way for the Way to reveal itself, and the more one *lives* the Way, the more the Way nourishes your spiritual self; and I *lived* Gurdjieff's teaching of "work on oneself; I *lived* Jesus Christ's sayings; I *lived* my *Royal Dictum* (my personal edict of self-denial); and I *lived* all of the wisdom sayings that I garnered from my daily life—which is how I could tap into the ineffable wisdom of Soul. (Incidentally, this is how I write all of my spiritual musings—*I just let go and let Soul speak!*)

In effect, it was my strange relationship with Kevin Archer that convinced me I had the gift of tapping into Soul consciousness; and so I decided to explore this gift and do a book by just *letting Soul speak.* This simply meant that I let go and let my higher self come through, which essentially is what all creative writers do when they write. That's how I created my book *The Way of Soul*, which Jung wanted to discuss with me in my dream.

My dream with Jung became central to my novel *The Waking Dream,* which was accepted by an American publisher but which I declined to proceed with because my editor and I did not have a meeting of minds; but all the same, my experience with C.G. Jung speaks to the way of Soul in the strange world of dreams—because Jung and I did talk about my book *The Way of Soul*, which was still a long way from being published yet!

So, what happened? Did I actually meet C.G. Jung in my dream? Or was he an archetypal manifestation of my own unconscious? That's the question that inspired today's spiritual musing—because I believe that both are true.

Carl Jung had a dream that puzzled him his whole life. He dreamt that he saw himself in a hillside chapel in a meditative posture dreaming his life as Carl Jung, and he *knew* that the man dreaming his life as Carl Jung was his real Self and that the psychiatrist called Carl Jung was his dream. In effect, *he knew that he was dreaming his own life!*

Jung's dream is reminiscent of the philosopher Chuang Tzu's famous dream: *"I dreamed I was a butterfly, flitting around in the sky; then I awoke. Now I wonder: Am I a man who dreamt of being a butterfly, or am I a butterfly dreaming that I am a man?"*

I had an experience that sheds light on both Jung's and Chuang Tzu's dream experiences. I woke up in my dream and became acutely aware of just how real everything was in my dream state. The reality of my dream state was a thousand times more real than my reality in my non-dream, physical state of consciousness; but I wanted to prove to myself which was the greater reality, so I woke up from my conscious dream experience to test my senses. I turned the light on in my bedroom and just sat on my bed and took in the reality of my physical state of consciousness, but it just didn't compare to the highly intensified reality of my dream state of consciousness; so I decided to go back to sleep and resume my dream state of consciousness, which I did. *I woke up again in my dream and concluded that my dream state of consciousness was more real than my physical state!*

The secret knowledge of dreams teaches that dreams are a gateway to the Other Side; meaning, the parallel worlds of other dimensions. These parallel worlds are the other planes of consciousness known as the Astral, Causal, Mental, and Soul Planes.

This is what I believed, and why my understanding of dreams had a tendency to always want to usurp the Jungian interpretation of dreams—until I had a new awakening and realized that each interpretation was just another face of the same reality!

I did meet Carl Jung on the Other Side in my dream, and Carl Jung was also an archetypal manifestation of the collective unconscious; but how can this be?

Jung came very close to answering this question. He wrote, "My life is a story of the self-realization of the unconscious." The unconscious for Jung was the unrealized Self, the central archetype of his psychology of individuation—what the whole evolutionary process of life was all about for him (and for me as well); that's why he came to me upon reading my book *The Way of Soul*, because he had a dying curiosity to know all about "the alpha and omega of the Self."

"What is the Self? Where does the Self come from? And where does the Self go?" he asked me in my dream, because he could not find a definite answer when he was alive; and we talked for hours. Maybe even longer than his legendary thirteen hour talk with Sigmund Freud upon first meeting face to face in Vienna (time on the Other Side is not relative to time on this side), and I woke up from my dream bursting with excitement because I was finally able to pay Jung back for the spiritual solace of his wisdom—especially his remarkable insights into the psychological nature of evil, which he called the personal and collective shadow.

Carl Jung came into my life to help me resolve my problem with my shadow and the concept of evil that my Roman Catholic faith had saddled me with, and I came into his life to help him resolve his problem of the Self; and we talked about what I called "the Divine Plan of God" in my as-yet unpublished book *The Way of Soul*.

Since I've already explored this in *The Waking Dream,* I need not expound upon it in today's spiritual musing; suffice to say that what Jung called the collective unconscious, I understood to be the unconscious state of Soul. And as Jung saw the collective unconscious forever in the process of individuating the Self, I saw Soul forever in the process of individuating the consciousness of its divine nature; and both interpretations were merely different facets of the same reality that complimented each other.

Jung saw dreams from a psychological perspective, and I saw dreams from a spiritual perspective, but both spoke to the same reality of the Divine Plan of God; and this reality is the essential purpose of life—which is to expand the consciousness of God by giving birth to a new "I" of God (what Jung calls the Self) through the evolution of life.

To answer Jung's three questions then: What is the Self? Answer: Soul. Where does the Self come from? Answer: The Self is a Soul seed, which is an un-self-realized atom of God that comes into the world from the Body of God to realize its divine nature. Where does the Self go? Answer: back to God a fully-realized Soul Self.

And if I may pose one final question: Is life real or a dream? Answer: to quote my mentor Gurdjieff: *"There is only self-initiation into the mysteries of life!"*

40. Does the World Need to Be Saved?

"Behold, be grateful, and forgive that which you did not understand and control. For life is divine, it is perfect, and it naturally manifests the will of its creator."

LOVE WITHOUT END, JESUS SPEAKS
By Glenda Green

Man's greatest fear today is the destruction of our world. We cannot turn on the TV and not hear some variation of man's fear, be it global warming, hurricanes, flooding, tsunamis, earthquakes, drought, economic breakdowns, political upheavals—all causes for keeping us in a fear state of consciousness; but are we heading for an apocalyptic disaster? Many people think so. And many people think the world needs to be saved.

I too used to think that the world needed to be saved; but from what? As coincidence would have it, yesterday morning when I began writing this musing, which is going to bring closure to my musings on "old whore life," Penny asked if I would accompany her to the clinic in Midland. She was going for a mammogram and blood work.

She needn't have asked, but because I knew they didn't have much reading material in the x-ray department where I had waited for Penny to get her foot x-rayed earlier in the month, I grabbed a magazine from my pile of unread magazines in my writing room, and for reasons known only to Providence I selected the Sept/Oct 2011issue of *Utne Reader*—which I learned in the waiting room just happened to have an article titled "Dispatches from the Apocalypse: What natural disasters reveal about our planet and its destiny"!

As I read the article while Penny had her mammogram, smiling to myself as I always do whenever I am blessed with another coincidence because I knew that by selecting that magazine at random Providence was telling me I was in sync with the rhythm of life with my closing musing on the question of whether the world needed to be saved or not, one line jumped out at me as if highlighted by the invisible Hand of God: **"Disasters don't just happen. They are always made possible by a series of often invisible social choices that implicate more than just those beings drowned or buried in rubble."**

Junot Diaz, the author of the article, analyzes the January 12, 2010 earthquake that struck Haiti to see what it was telling the world. He writes: "I cannot contemplate the apocalypse of Haiti without asking the question: Where is all this leading? Where are the patterns and forces that we have set in motion in our world—the patterns and forces that made Haiti's devastation not only possible but inevitable—delivering us? To what end, to what future, to what fate?"

I finished reading the article with a heavy sigh, not because of the bleak picture that Junot Diaz had painted of man's blind capacity for self-destruction, but because he had confirmed the central theme of my closing spiritual musing—*that the world is what it is because of the choices man makes; and only by changing the values that we live by can we change the world.* But man is a creature of habit, which is why Junot Diaz was not as hopeful of the outcome of the world's fate as he would have liked.

This article answered my question "what does the world need to be saved from?" It has to be saved from man's spiritual ignorance, which is responsible for the fate of the world. And herein lies my quandary—because my life-long quest for the meaning and purpose of life has brought me to the Divine Plan of God, which offers us the understanding that the world is what it is for the specific purpose of giving man the opportunity to evolve into spiritually self-realized beings; and for this to happen man must experience life in all of its manifestations, both good and evil. Which means that from this perspective the world does not need to be saved, as such; it simply needs to be understood.

Of course this doesn't mean that we should simply resign ourselves to what Diaz and most people think will be the inevitable destruction of our world; on the contrary, we should strive to improve the conditions of the world—because in our efforts to make the world a better place, we fulfill our spiritual purpose in life. And this is exactly what Andrew Harvey is doing with the movement he founded called "Sacred Activism."

I discovered Andrew Harvey by "chance" when Providence introduced me to the Jungian analyst Marion Woodman in the television documentary "Dancing in the Flames," which was based on Marion Woodman's life. Andrew Harvey interviewed Marion in this documentary, and he was such a fascinating man that I went on the Internet and researched his life and discovered "Sacred Activism." But he was so unbelievably passionate whenever he spoke about saving the world from inevitable destruction that I had to sit back and smile yet again at how the Holy Flame of God works in life.

The Holy Flame of God is the redemptive power of Holy Spirit that reconciles man with his spiritual destiny; or, to put it simply, brings man into agreement with himself and God. In effect, the Holy Flame of God is the Spirit of the Way; and when one becomes possessed by the Spirit of the Way he can become so consumed by the Holy Flame of God that he will be driven to not only save himself, but the world—just as Andrew Harvey is doing.

The Holy Flame of God has puzzled the world, and not until one becomes consumed by the reconciling power of God's Love will he understand what it means to be possessed by the Spirit of the Way. I became possessed by the Spirit of the Way when I began to "work" on myself with Gurdjieff's teaching; and the more I "worked" on myself, the more possessed I became—to the point where I also wanted to save the world!

But I was very, very lucky to have Gurdjieff as my mentor—because he made me take a vow of silence about "working" on myself. This was the condition that he imposed upon me to become a member of his inner circle on the Other Side.

Gurdjieff was long dead when I met him in my dreams. The first time I met him I begged him to take me into his inner circle, but he said I wasn't ready. But after two years of "working" on myself with the self-transformative principles of his teaching, I met him again in my dreams and he accepted me into his inner circle—but only if I took a vow of silence, which he explained would not only provide me with an incredible store of energy to "create" my own soul, but it would also protect me from an incredulous world.

I took the vow of silence; and the more I "worked" on myself under his dream-guidance, the more I became consumed by the Holy Flame of God. And the more consumed I became, the more I wanted to save the world; but I couldn't. And now I am ever so grateful for my vow of silence, because saving the world is not for everybody.

But saving oneself is…

Plus an Interview with the Author and More

INSIGHTS

*"A little sincerity is a dangerous thing,
and a great deal of it is absolutely fatal."*

Oscar Wilde

Man's willful blindness to his own shadow self in a world where the collective shadow of the world is wreaking ineluctable havoc is man's greatest challenge, and man's only salvation is to wake up to his paradoxical predicament; but how?

The answer is obvious: man must resolve the conflicting archetypal forces of his own shadow self. But to do this man has to become aware of his shadow. This is why I wrote my musings on "old whore life," to acquaint readers with the most repressed aspect of our personality—or, if you will, the "old whore" faces of our shadow self.

"Old whore life" has many faces, and just when we think we have come to terms with our shadow self we get another surprise, as I have repeatedly shown in my musings on "old whore life". But why do I persist on calling our shadow self an "old whore"? Is it fair to the archetypal feminine principle of life? Is it fair to my own anima?

It's not really a question of fairness. It's more a question of trying to understand ourselves. A writer writes to get to the truth of life, and we use imagination to magnify our perceptions of reality so we can get a better picture of life. It's easy enough to see our outer life, but not so easy to see our inner life; that's why I personified our shadow self as an old whore that loves to screw us of our virtue. I wanted to freeze-frame our shadow in action.

But we can only understand our shadow in the context of our essential purpose in life, which is to become aware of our divine nature. We grow and evolve in self-consciousness within the parameters of karma and reincarnation, and when we have grown enough through the natural process of creating and resolving karma we realize that we are the authors of our own destiny and feel compelled to make better karmic choices; and a better karmic choice would be one that does not create negative karma.

When we make choices that create negative karma we feed our shadow, which can grow to the point where it can take over our ego self—like the Doctor Jekyll and Mr. Hyde story. Mr. Hyde was Doctor Jekyll's shadow self, and it came out and took over Doctor Jekyll's personality. This is the mysterious nature of the human psyche, and it is not easy to see our own Mr. Hyde. Like Carl Jung said, it takes great moral courage to see our own shadow. But we cannot realize our destiny if we do not resolve the karma of our shadow self; which means that we carry our shadow energy from one life to the next.

This does not paint a nice picture of the shadow. But like the portrait of Dorian Gray, we can ask: who was responsible for the way the portrait looked? Dorian Gray himself was responsible, because every time he committed a sin it manifested in his portrait.

When Wilde wrote *The Picture of Dorian Gray* he employed the creative powers of his imagination to freeze-frame the shadow in Dorian Gray's portrait. Although all of Dorian Gray's sins did not show up in his physical appearance (which is why he stayed so young looking as he grew older) they showed up in his portrait hidden away in a locked room—just like our shadow that is hidden in the unconscious regions of our psyche.

If you will, then; I have painted a portrait of our shadow self just as Robert Louis Stevenson painted his portrait of Mr. Hyde, and Oscar Wilde painted his portrait of Dorian Gray; and as difficult as it was to freeze-frame the shadow in the image "old whore life," I hope my musings will help to better understand that we are the authors of our own karma, and only we can change our destiny. So if life continues to "screw" us of our virtue, we have no one to blame but ourselves; for such is the mystery of "old whore life."

PREVIEW OF COMING WORK

<u>JESUS WEARS DOCKERS</u>

THE MESSIAH SECRET REVEALED

A Novel

By Orest Stocco

Chapter 1

Let the World Find Its Own Way

I felt a gentle tap on my shoulder. I turned to look. It was Jesus. "Did you enjoy the service?" he asked, with a bright twinkle in his eyes.

"As a matter of fact, it was the most satisfying service I've attended yet," I replied, smiling with surprise. "I'm glad you appeared, because I had serious doubts about attending any more worship services."

Jesus did not say anything, but his eyes beckoned me.

"Tell me, Jesus," I said, as though talking to an old friend, "is it me, or is what I'm witnessing a clear picture of the conceit that I see in these Higher Initiates?"

"Both," replied Jesus, with a smile. "You have to appreciate where they're coming from, even if they have no idea of the effect they have on people. Not all of them, of course. Just those Higher Initiates that have not yet resolved the deeper issues of their own vanity."

"It is a curse, isn't it?"

"What, vanity?"

"Yes."

"Tell me about it. Even on the cross I preened like a peacock!"

I burst into laughter. "You certainly fooled a lot of people," I said, still laughing at Christ's surprising candor. "But not the Living Soul Master. He saw through the vanity of your mission to save the world and called you the boldest of peacocks. But that's all water under the bridge, isn't it? So, what are you doing here now?"

"How can I put this?" Jesus said, furrowing his brow. I looked at him, smiling at the contrast that the real Jesus made with the image the world has drawn of its savior. A small, slender man not more than five feet one or two inches tall, Jesus was still dressed in the same casual wear that he had on when he miraculously appeared at our worship service at the public library: a warm yellow short-sleeve polo shirt and a pair of tan Dockers just like the ones Cathy had purchased for me a couple of weeks earlier, and a pair of sandals on his bare feet. Jesus was clean shaven, but his face was not what I imagined. It was broad, full jowled, and although striking it was not what one would call handsome. It was angular, and quite distinctive, but it wasn't his face that my eyes fell upon first; it was his eyes. Jesus had the most striking hazelnut eyes that shone with such clarity it felt like looking into the barrier reef of his soul, which was infinite in its beauty. And his short brown hair was cut in a modish style that gave him a young, professorial look. In fact, his whole presence gave me the feeling that we were old alumni of the Way taking a leisurely stroll through the campus of life. "It's time to set the record straight," he finally said, which gave me a feeling of regret that it had taken him this long to reveal the messiah secret. I had decided to stretch my legs and walk to the park several blocks from the library to reflect on my other-worldly experience with Jesus earlier at the service when he surprised me again with a tap on my shoulder. "The world has greatly misunderstood my teaching," he continued, with obvious remorse in his voice, "and you can help me to set the record straight."

I felt the strangest presentiment, like I was about to enter once again into another parallel world. I couldn't speak for a moment or two. "Why me?" I finally asked.

"Need I tell you?" Jesus said, his face lighting up with so much love that I actually felt it touching me like a strong draft of warm air.

I was compelled to smile. Suddenly, I broke into a fit of giddy laughter as Holy Spirit rushed into me with such incredible force that I could not contain the electric joy of two souls connecting with the Holy Current of God. "You don't have to tell me," I replied, feeling the strongest urge to grab Jesus and give him a big hug. "But I'd sure love to hear you say it," I quickly added, to my own amazement.

Jesus laughed. I felt embarrassed for revealing my emotions.

"Alright, O," he said, with the sweetest smile on his remarkable face. "I'll firm up your confidence for you, if you like. You have proven to be an exceptional channel for the true spirit of my sayings which have puzzled the world far too long, and I need your help to set the record straight.

Would you be interested in having a dialogue with me to explain the secret of spiritual rebirth in my gospel to the world?"

"Finally!" I exclaimed, once again to my amazement. I felt like I was so far outside myself that I wasn't even the same person. *"What the hell took you so long?"* I instantly added, and burst into another fit of giddy laughter.

Jesus laughed also. And the more we laughed, the more light-headed I felt. "I have to sit down," I said. "I feel dizzy—"

"There's a bench," Jesus pointed, and walked over and sat down. I staggered over and flopped down. The moment I got off my feet my dizziness went away.

"What was it you asked?" I said. I still felt giddy with love. I looked at Jesus and laughed again. His energy was too much for me all at once.

"That's what divine love can do to a person when two souls connect," Jesus said.

"Yes. I understand. I've always associated laughter with love. And yet, the world has come to see you as a humorless savior. Why is that, J?" I asked, but with such surprising familiarity that it set free another bout of giddy laughter.

"These are difficult times, and the world needs more humor today," he said, with that same feeling of camaraderie in his voice that had just overwhelmed me. "This is why I need your help to set the record straight. You have the right spirit, O."

"Set the record straight?" I said, as the most vivid image of the most crooked path in the world flashed across my mind. *"We couldn't set Christianity straight if we had the faith of a trillion mustard seeds!"*

Jesus broke into a fit of irrepressible laughter. He had to hold his stomach. "Probably not," he finally said, once again with the sweetest smile on his exceptional face. "But I'd sure like to try all the same, O."

Sobering up at the serious tone of his voice, I collected myself and replied, "It's the Way of Christ that you want to explain to the world?"

"Exactly," said Jesus.

"And what consequences can I expect for helping you?" I asked, feeling the gravity of his request. "Another malicious rebuff from the world? If you don't know it yet, J, as far as I'm concerned the world can find its own way—*and I mean that!"*

Jesus smiled. "I know you do, O. This is why I have chosen you. You are the right man for this task. You have just the right attitude to help put my gospel teaching into proper perspective. This is why Stanley Hansen has difficulty with you. And other chelas. It's your attitude, O. I love it, but it's too much for most people."

"Why is that?" I had to ask. Jesus was referring to my relationship with my spiritual community. From the day Cathy and I moved to Georgian Bay I felt an underlying tension with my fellow chelas, but I couldn't explain it.

"You chafe people, O. You have a way of pricking their vanity," Jesus explained. "Some chelas have difficulty accepting how you treat the teachings of the Light and Sound of God like any other spiritual path. It's a blow to their spiritual conceit."

"But that's only because I know that life is the Way!"
I heard myself shouting at Jesus. *"O vanity of vanities, all is vanity!"* I added, feeling very defensive.

"Exactly!" Jesus exclaimed, to my surprise. "This is why I want to dialogue with you on my gospel teaching. We're both Initiates of the Way. With your help, I can finally set the record of my gospel straight. What do you say, O? Are you up to the challenge?"

Again, sobering up at Christ's tone I felt myself suddenly centered, and replied, "By gospel, you're referring to your sayings?"

"Essentially, yes. It's in my sayings that my gospel can be found."

"And it doesn't really matter if you authored these sayings or not, does it?" I said, and then suddenly broke into another fit of laughter at the image of an endless line of hunch-backed monks leaning over their Bible baffling over Christ's enigmatic sayings.

"Precisely!" Jesus burst out, with such force in his voice that it brought me back to myself. *"The gospel of Christ is the Way of Life! The Way of Life is the Way! And the Way exists in all the sayings of life, because the Way is life itself!"* Jesus added, with such intensity that I centered completely. "This is why I need your help, O. Too much has been made of who said this and who said that. What does it matter if one angel or ten billion angels can stand on the head of a pin, or if you live one life or a thousand lives? This is just another one of *Deus Deceptor's* little games to keep Soul trapped in the lower worlds. You have broken through this barrier, O. You know that life is the Way. You speak the language of the Way. And you know my teaching as well as the Gospel writers. What do you say, O? Are you

up to the challenge?" Jesus asked, almost like he was pleading with me.

I couldn't believe my ears. I had to chuckle to relieve the pressure of Christ's words; but I did relish the idea of helping the messiah of the world reveal his secret.

"I see where you're coming from," I said, feeling totally myself now. "As a matter of fact," I added as the memory surfaced, "I anticipated this dialogue with you fifteen years ago with a book that I wanted to write. I was going to call it *The Meat of the Last Supper.*"

Jesus burst into laughter again. The infectious spirit of joy possessed me once more, and I giggled with light-headed abandon.

"What do you say, O? Are you up to the challenge of helping me to dispel the Gospel conspiracy?" Jesus asked, with just the right edge to provoke me.

"Gospel conspiracy? What Gospel conspiracy?" I asked, puzzled.

Jesus looked me deep in the eyes. It was the first time I saw it, but there was the subtlest hint of a playful mischievousness in his eyes and curve of his lips that I would come to see often in the course of our talks, not unlike the mystic Mona Lisa's smile that teased my sense of reality. "You'll come to see what I mean in good time," he replied.

"What the hell!" I burst out, surprising myself. *"Why not?"*

"Good!" said Jesus, and gave me a friendly slap on the shoulder.

"You know, J," I said, feeling his love filling me up again so quickly that I could not contain it, "that's the problem with the spiritual life today—*not enough whimsy!"*

"You won't regret this, O. I promise you," Jesus said, with the biggest grin.

"Please, no promises! I couldn't stand to be disappointed in you again!" I said, and broke into another fit of giddy laughter.

Jesus joined me, and we laughed to our heart's content like two old friends who hadn't seen each other in many, many years.

THE MAKING OF A SPIRITUAL MEMOIR

It was innocent enough, the question that Lorie asked Oriano in my novel *Healing with Padre Pio.* Oriano told Lorie that mastering the art of giving love was the most difficult thing in the world to do, and Lorie replied: "If it's so difficult, why would one bother?" Oriano told Lorie she could find the answer to this riddle in the Parable of the Good Samaritan; but I don't know why Oriano told her that. That's why I had to write *Why Bother? The Riddle of the Good Samaritan*.

Despite the fact that Oriano was my fictional self, I had no idea that he would tell Lorie she could find her answer in the Parable of the Good Samaritan, because Oriano was a character in his own right who spoke with his own voice.

But as independent as Oriano was, he was born of my soul as Eve was born of Adam's rib; so I knew the answer to the riddle, and I had to tease it out of myself by telling the story of how I came to the conclusion that mastering the art of giving love was the most difficult thing in the world to do; hence the making of a spiritual memoir.

No two souls have the same *karmic destiny*, so everyone's journey through life is different. *Memories, Dreams, Reflections* is Carl Jung's spiritual memoir; just as *The Inspired Heart, An Artist's Journey of Transformation* is Jerry Wennstrom's spiritual memoir; and *Crossing the*

Unknown Sea, Work as a Pilgrimage of Identity is David Whyte's spiritual memoir, so is *Why Bother? The Riddle of the Good Samaritan* my spiritual memoir, because as Jung, Wennstrom, and Whyte had to forge their own path in life so too did I have to forge mine.

A spiritual memoir is the sacred story of one's relationship with God. Jung's, Wennstrom's, and Whyte's relationship with God are all unique to the individual, as is every soul's; but they all have one thing in common—a longing for God, which can only be satisfied through the *individuation process* of one's own way; and finding one's own way is what a spiritual memoir is all about.

I didn't realize it when I began my quest for my true self, but my quest was nothing less than seeking a way to satisfy my longing for God because my true self was a spark of divine consciousness that longed to realize itself. **"I and my Father are one,"** said Jesus, as is every soul one with God the Father; but not every soul realizes this. This is the secret of Christ's teaching of *eternal life*: how to satisfy our longing for God.

In the *Gospel of Thomas* Jesus said, **"Whoever finds the interpretation of these sayings will not taste death,"** and in the Parable of the Good Samaritan he tells the lawyer that if he wanted to *inherit eternal life* he had to love his neighbor; meaning, he would have to grow in the consciousness of *eternal life* to realize his *eternal life*, and the only way to grow in the consciousness of *eternal life* was to love his fellow man—which Jesus knew would not be easy because it would go against his primal selfish nature to give love to his fellow man; that's why mastering the art of giving love is the most difficult thing in the world to do.

My spiritual memoir is the story of how I became aware of my primal selfish nature, how I wrestled myself free from the hold it had over me, and how I learned to transform my selfish nature and grow in the consciousness of *eternal life*; and I did this by "working" on myself with Gurdjieff's teaching, my *Royal Dictum* (my personal edict of self-denial inspired by Sophocles' play *Oedipus Rex*), and Christ's sayings.

In effect, I forged my own path to my true self by individuating the consciousness of the Way that I found concentrated in Gurdjieff's teaching and Christ's sayings; and the Way is Divine Spirit, which is the life force and omniscient guiding force of life that exists everywhere—like in the Parable of the Good Samaritan.

This is why I had to write *Why Bother? The Riddle of the Good Samaritan,* because it was my entry point into the mystery of the omniscient guiding force of life that is everywhere to be found; and, if I may be allowed to say so, it is my gesture of love to all the seekers stranded by the side of the road on their journey home to God.

AN INTERVIEW WITH THE AUTHOR

Conducted by my editor Penny Lynn Cates

P: *Old Whore Life: Exploring the Shadow Side of Karma* is the second volume of your spiritual musings. You introduced this book in your blog first, but some readers were disturbed by the concept of old whore life. Do you think it was too much for them?

O: Let me ask you a question: how do you think a woman would feel if an old friend told her that she was looking a little frumpy since the last time he saw her?

P: I think she would be offended. But why hurt her feelings?

O: He's a man, and men can be insensitive when it comes to women. But is there a sensitive way to tell the truth about life? That was my dilemma. Writers are truth tellers. This is why we write fiction. A case in point would be Oscar Wilde. He wrote a novel called *The Picture of Dorian Gray.* This novel is an insight into man's soul, not unlike *Faust* by Goethe. Faust bargained his soul to the Devil. Oscar Wilde used the metaphor of a portrait painting to illustrate the image of one man's compromised soul, that man being

Dorian Gray. Wilde used the craft of fiction to reveal the truth about the shadow side of human nature, just as Robert Louis Stevenson did with his novel *The Strange Case of Dr. Jekyll and Mr. Hyde.* Stevenson revealed the dark shadow side of Dr. Jekyll's personality. I did the same thing. I wanted to capture the shadow side of the human personality, and I employed the metaphor of an old whore to give it a face. But just as Mr. Hyde was not a pleasant person, nor was the portrait of Dorian Gray pleasant to look at, neither is the image of old whore life. She's not very pleasant, but like it or not she is the hidden side of our nature; that's why some readers were disturbed. They didn't want to see their own shadow side.

P: Yes, but if a woman looks frumpy that's because she is frumpy. Why would you want to hurt her feelings by pointing out the obvious?

O: Great question. The strange thing about the shadow side of our personality is that it's obvious to others but not to ourselves. This is why it can be so disturbing when we stare into the face of our own shadow. For example, I had no idea that I was so full of myself until I went for a spiritual healing last year. This is what my novel *Healing with Padre Pio* is all about—my journey through vanity to humility. I would never have seen the depths of my own vanity had not St. Padre Pio held up a mirror for me to see myself. That's all I'm doing with my spiritual musings, holding up a mirror for my readers to see their shadow.

OLD WHORE LIFE

P: I know that karma is the spiritual law of cause and effect, but I still can't wrap my head around what you mean by the shadow side of karma?

O: You've heard the old saying, *what goes around comes around*? This implies that what we do to others is going to happen to us one day. We may not make the connection when it happens to us, because more often than not we have forgotten what we did to deserve what happens to us. For example, suppose I break a woman's heart. I'm married, and I lead another woman on, letting her believe that I will leave my wife for her; but one day she realizes that I'm not going to leave my wife and it breaks her heart. Now suppose that my wife falls in love with another man and wants a divorce. I love my wife, despite the fact that I had an affair with another woman, and it breaks my heart when she leaves me for another man. That's karma in action. *What goes around comes around.* I drew a clear picture to make my point, but karma is very, very subtle. I wanted to show the subtle side of karma. I called it the shadow side of karma, because that's what it is. It's the hidden side of our selfish nature, which we don't want to see. If we see it we have to take responsibility for it, and who wants to admit that they are their own old whore and author of their own misery? I spell this out clearly in my spiritual musing "Old Whore Life, *C'est moi.*"

P: Did you enjoy writing *Old Whore Life*?

O: Yes and no. I enjoyed exploring the shadow side of karma because I love catching the devil by the tail, but it cost me to shine the spotlight on old whore life.

P: In what way?

O: I don't know if I can explain this. It's very metaphysical. But I'll try. Writing this book made me very, very angry at life. For the longest time I could not figure out where all my anger was coming from, but finally it dawned on me. Every time I posted a new spiritual musing on old whore life on my blog, I made my reader a little more conscious of the shadow side of their personality, and this made their shadow very angry at me because the shadow does not want to be seen. The shadow wants to be out, but not seen; that's why the shadow's greatest fear is the light of consciousness. So the more light I shed on old whore life, the angrier the Archetypal Shadow was with me. The Archetypal Shadow is the collective shadow side of man, which I personified as old whore life, and the more I revealed the old whore in my weekly blog the more I felt her anger. But my Muse wanted this book out there, so I had to see it through. And what a relief it was when it was finished. That's when my anger began to go away.

P: Are you going to write another book of spiritual musings?

O: Yes. I'm going to focus on the warrior within this time. I want to see if I can awaken the noble side of man's nature. My entry point is Wordsworth's poem "Character of the Happy Warrior." *"Who is the Happy Warrior? Who is he that every man in arms should wish to be?"* asks Wordsworth. *"It is the generous Spirit..."* That's what I'm going to explore in my third volume of spiritual musings—the generous spirit of man's noble nature.

P: How about *Healing with Padre Pio*? Are you going to write a sequel?

O: I hope to. *Healing with Padre Pio* opened up a new world for me, and I've already begun my research. St. Padre Pio told me something about myself that blew my mind: he said that I'm living my same life over again to obtain a different outcome. This means that I'm living in a parallel world this time around. This is what I'm exploring with my new book, *The Summoning of Noman*. But that's not my sequel to *Healing with Padre Pio*. That's another project, which I'll be doing with the psychic who channeled St. Padre Pio.

P: What do you mean by parallel world?

O: This is where spirituality meets science. Science has finally caught up to the ancient spiritual traditions of the world, which posit the existence of a multi-dimensional universe; but that's a big topic, and I'd rather wait until I do some more research. I've already begun my research with Gregg Braden's books. He's bridging science with ancient spiritual traditions like the Essene, Buddhist, and native traditions with books like *The Isaiah Effect*, *The Divine Matrix*, and *The God Code*.

P: Where do you think your research will take you?

O: Believe it or not, it's taking me back to a deeper study of dreams. Dreams are a gateway to parallel worlds, so I've started keeping a new dream journal to research dream consciousness. St. Padre Pio told me that *life is a journey of the self*. He also told me that *life is a voyage of discovery*. And finally, he told me that our *life is a journey of peace*. I think my research will cover all three categories, hopefully ending with some measure of peace that I can share with my reader. Life really is a mystery, and we will never have peace of mind until we solve it. That's my hope.

Other Books by Orest Stocco

Why Bother? The Riddle of the Good Samaritan
Healing with Padre Pio
Just Going With the Flow, And Other Spiritual Musings
Keeper of the Flame
My Unborn Child
What Would I Say Today If I Were To Die Tomorrow?
On the Wings of Habitat, A Volunteer's Story

Coming Works

Jesus Wears Dockers: The Messiah Secret Revealed
The Seeker: Quest for the Lost Soul of God
The Waking Dream

About the Author

Orest Stocco was born in Panettieri, Calabria, Italy. He emigrated to Canada and studied philosophy at university. A student of Gurdjieff's teaching for many years which opened him up to the Way, his passion for writing inspired such innovative works as *What Would I Say Today If I Were To Die Tomorrow?*, *Keeper of the Flame,* and *Healing with Padre Pio.* He lives in Georgian Bay, Ontario with his life mate Penny Lynn Cates. His personal dictum is: *life is an individual journey.* Visit him at:

http://www.oreststocco.com

Spiritual Musings Blogs:

http://www.spiritualmusingsbyoreststocco.blogspot.com

http://www.letterstoascendedmasterstpadrepio.blogspot.com

ME AND MY SISPYHEAN ROCK